A
Wizard's
Dozen

A Wizard's Dozen

Stories of the Fantastic

EDITED BY

MICHAEL STEARNS

A Jane Yolen Book

Harcourt Brace & Company

San Diego   New York   London

Library of Congress Cataloging-in-Publication Data
A Wizard's dozen/edited by Michael Stearns.
    p.   cm.
"Jane Yolen books."
Contents: The Sixty-Two Curses of Caliph Arenschadd/Patricia C.
Wrede—Fairy dust/Charles de Lint—The Princess Who Kicked
Butt/Will Shetterly—The sea giants/Betty Levin—Efrum's
marbles/Joy Oestreicher—"Come hither"/Tappan King—The
Queen's mirror/Debra Doyle and James D. Macdonald—The breath of
princes/Alan P. Smale—Harlyn's Fairy/Jane Yolen—Lost soul/
Vivian Vande Velde—The way of prophets/Dan Bannett—Faith/
Sherwood Smith—With his head tucked underneath his arm/Bruce
Coville.
ISBN 0-15-200965-5 (hc).   ISBN 0-15-200966-3 (pbk.)
1. Fantastic fiction. 2. Children's stories.
[1. Fantasy. 2. Short stories.]
I. Stearns, Michael.
PZ5.W7568 1993
[Fic]—dc20   93-22150

Printed in the United States of America
First edition
A B C D E

For my mother, Louise Magella Maheu

wizard's dozen \ 'wiz-ə(r)dz 'dəz-ən\   **1** : any magical number from eleven to fifteen   **2** : the charmed numeral that gives a wizard's spell its power   **3** : the number of teachers at a wizards' school

Contents

To the Reader

What is a wizard?

A wizard is a mage, a wonder maker, a person who injects a jolt of the marvelous into the everyday. There are wizards everywhere, though these days they've traded in their magic shops and their spellbooks for libraries and storybooks. Today's wizards wield paintbrushes or pens or typewriters or computers instead of wands.

Some may have long white beards, but most do not. Today's wizards come in all ages, all genders, all colors and shapes. They are the authors and artists who work with stories of the fantastic. What they have is vision, and—most importantly—they can share that vision with others. They enable us all to see a little farther, to see a little deeper.

It is no small gift.

Some people, recognizing the power of these everyday mages, try to limit the magic. They try to keep the magic out of their lives. So they rail against the malicious influence of certain kinds of literature. They denigrate it, remove it from their libraries. In other words, they ban it.

The fantasy stories in this collection could all be labeled "escapist literature." But fantasy is rarely as much of an escape as its detractors would have us believe. In fantasy stories — in the stories in this book, in fact — we learn to understand the differences of others, we learn compassion for those things we cannot fathom, we learn the importance of keeping our sense of wonder. The strange worlds that exist in the pages of fantastic literature teach us a tolerance of other people and places and engender an openness toward new experience. Fantasy books put the world into perspective in a way that "realistic" literature rarely does. It is not so much an escape from the here-and-now as an expansion of each reader's horizons.

Most importantly, these tales can open us up to the pleasure and delight of the imagination.

Mage — image — imagination.

That is magic enough for any wizard.

A Wizard's Dozen

PATRICIA C. WREDE

The Sixty-two Curses of Caliph Arenschadd

The worst thing about Caliph Arenschadd is that he's a wizard. At least that's what my father says. Mother says the worst thing about the caliph is his temper, and that it's a good thing he's a wizard because if he were just an ordinary caliph he'd cut people's heads off when they displeased him, instead of cursing them.

I tend to agree with Mother. Cutting someone's head off is permanent; a curse, you can break. Of course, it usually takes something nasty and undignified to do it, but everything about curses is supposed to be unpleasant. Father doesn't see it that way. I think he'd prefer to be permanently dead than temporarily undignified.

Father is Caliph Arenschadd's grand vizier, which is the reason all of us have opinions about the caliph and his curses. You see, a long time ago the caliph decided that he would lay a curse on anyone who displeased him, thus punishing the person and displaying the caliph's magical skill at the same time. (Mother also says Caliph Arenschadd likes to show off.) He found out very quickly that it was hard work coming up with a new curse every time someone made him unhappy, but by then he'd had a proclamation issued and he couldn't back down. So he shut himself up in one of the palace minarets for weeks, and when he came out he had a list of sixty-two curses he could cast at a moment's notice.

From then on, every time someone has done something the caliph doesn't like, the caliph has hauled out his list of curses and slapped one on whoever-it-was. Everyone starts at the first curse on the list and works their way down, so you can tell how long someone's been at court by whether his fingernails are three feet long or his eyelids stuck together. Father's been at court longer than anybody, so we've worked our way through an awful lot of curses.

I say *we* because Caliph Arenschadd doesn't just curse the particular person he's annoyed with. His curses get the person's whole family as well. I don't think that's fair, but Mother says it's just like him.

She's been mad at the caliph ever since the eleventh curse, which made all three of us lose our voices for a week right in the middle of the Enchantresses and Sorceresses Annual Conference. Mother was supposed to present a paper, but she had to cancel it because she couldn't talk, and she's never forgiven Caliph Arenschadd.

I have to admit that some of the curses are fun. I enjoyed being bright green, and having monkey's paws was quite useful (I like climbing things, and the peaches had just turned ripe). Having my eyelids stuck together was boring, though. Things even out. It's best when you know what to expect, but after Father passed the forty-second curse there wasn't anyone ahead of us anymore to let us know what came next. We muddled through curses number forty-three through forty-seven with only a little more trouble than usual, and Caliph Arenschadd actually seemed pleased. We went for almost three months without any curses at all. Then one day Father came home from the palace looking grim and solemn.

Mother took one look at him and said, "O my husband and light of my eyes, not *again!*" in the exasperated tone she usually saves for me when I've put a rip in my skirts.

"I'm afraid so, Mirza," Father said. "He was in an awful mood today, but I simply couldn't put off asking him about those water rights for the caravaners any longer. So we're going to find out about number forty-eight." Father never says the word *curse* when he's talking about one of Caliph Arenschadd's; he only refers to them by number.

"Someone should take that caliph in hand," Mother said.

"Are you offering?" Father demanded.

I could tell there was an argument starting, so I got up and slipped out of the room before they could get me in on it. Mother and Father usually have an argument right after Caliph Arenschadd puts another curse on us; I think it relieves their feelings or something. It never lasts long, and as soon as they're finished they start looking for the way to break the curse. They're very good at it. Most of the curses last less than a week, and the longest one only went nine days. It's never much fun to be around for the arguing part, though, which is why I left.

I went to visit my best friend, Tumpkin. Tumpkin isn't his real name; I call him that because the first time I met him he wouldn't tell me who he was and I had to call him something. I ran into him in one of the private gardens at the palace, so I figured he was one of the caliph's pages, poking around where he wasn't supposed to be. He's about the same age as I am, and he's nearsighted and sort of pudgy—just the kind of kid that gets picked on all the time. That's why I started calling him Tumpkin; it seemed to fit.

I didn't have to spend much time looking for Tumpkin on the first day of the forty-eighth curse. He was in his favorite spot, under a bush behind a gold garden seat. He heard me coming and looked up. When he saw who it was, he grinned at me in relief. "Imani!" he said. "I was just thinking about you."

"You ought to be thinking about your duties," I told him. "Someone's going to catch you shirking one of these days, and then you'll really be in trouble."

"Do *you* have to tell me what to do, too?" Tumpkin said grumpily. He waved in the direction of the palace. "You sound just like everyone in there."

"No, I sound like my father," I said, flopping down on the bench. "Sorry, it's been a rough day."

Tumpkin stopped looking grumpy and looked interested and sympathetic instead. "What happened?"

"Father picked up another curse, and he and Mother are arguing about it," I said.

"Another one?" Tumpkin said. "How many does that make?"

"Forty-eight," I said gloomily. "And we don't have even a tiny hint of what it is this time."

"I could try and find out for you," Tumpkin offered diffidently.

"Don't bother," I said. "Caliph Arenschadd takes better care of his list of curses than he does of the crown jewels. If you got caught, he'd probably slap four or five curses on you at once."

"He can't," Tumpkin said smugly. "They only work one at a time. And besides—"

"It's all *right*, Tumpkin," I said hastily. "We'll find out soon enough what number forty-eight is; you don't have to risk moving yourself up the list."

"Well, actually—" Tumpkin said, and stopped, looking very uncomfortable.

"Tumpkin!" I said, staring at him. "Do you mean to say the caliph has never put *any* of his curses on you?"

"I guess so," Tumpkin said. "I mean, no, he hasn't."

"You must be really good at keeping out of the

way," I said with considerable admiration. "I've never heard of anyone who didn't make it through at least five curses during his first six weeks at court, and you've been around for nearly a year!"

"Longer than that, but I spend a lot of time out here." Tumpkin sounded more uncomfortable than ever, so I let the subject drop and went back to talking about my parents and curse number forty-eight. After a while Tumpkin relaxed, but he didn't make a second offer to sneak a look at Caliph Arenschadd's list of curses.

I stayed with Tumpkin for most of the afternoon, and there was still no sign of the curse when I started for home. That worried me. The longer Caliph Arenschadd's curses take to have an effect, the nastier they tend to be. I could tell that Mother and Father were worried, too; neither of them said much at dinner.

That evening I had the first dream. I was running and running through the night, and the wind was in my hair, and a silver moon shone high in the sky. I woke up just as I realized that I was running on four feet, like a dog. The thin crescent of the waxing moon was framed in the window at the foot of my bed. I sat staring at it for a long time before I fell asleep again.

I had the same dream the following night. I didn't worry about it much at the time; I was far more concerned about the forty-eighth curse. There still didn't seem to be any signs of it taking hold, at least none that I could see, and I'd never known one of Caliph Arenschadd's curses to take this long to affect someone. I stayed inside most of the time, figuring that I'd rather not have to try to get home with my feet turned backward or my knees stuck together if the curse hit all of a sudden. I didn't even go to the palace to see Tumpkin.

Two nights later, the dream got stronger. I ran and ran, with the wind down my back and the ground flowing past my feet and the sweet smell of grass at night in my nostrils. And a silver moon hung round and perfect in the sky above me.

I dreamed again the following night, and every night after that. Always it was the same dream, of running strong and free and wild in the wind and the moonlight. And always I woke with the moon shining through the window at the foot of my bed. At first it was just a crescent-shaped sliver of silver light, but every day the sliver grew wider. My dream became more and more vivid as the moon waxed, until I could close my eyes even in the day and see moonlight shining on sharp blades of grass. I began looking forward to the night, because I knew that then I would dream of running in the wind.

I didn't tell anyone about the dream. Mother and Father were still puzzling over the curse, and I didn't want to distract them. Besides, the dream was a private, special thing. I didn't want to share it with anyone, not even Tumpkin.

Not that I'd been seeing much of Tumpkin. At first I didn't go to the palace because I didn't want the curse to catch up with me while I was away from home. By the time I decided I didn't care about the curse, I didn't want to go anywhere. I probably would have stayed home forever if Mother hadn't chased me out after a week so she could work on some delicate enchantments.

Tumpkin was glad to see me. In fact, he practically

pounced on me the minute I came into the garden. "You're back!" he said. "Did your parents figure out how to break it already? What was it, anyway?"

"What was what?" I asked crossly.

"The forty-eighth curse," Tumpkin said. He frowned worriedly at me. "Don't you remember?"

"Of course I remember!" I snapped. "No, Mother and Father haven't broken it, because they still don't know what it is."

"They don't know?"

"That's what I said. Didn't you listen? I think they should give up. If nothing's happened yet, the curse probably didn't take and we don't have anything to worry about."

"Something's happened," Tumpkin muttered.

"What did you say?" I said. "Why are you staring at me like that?"

"I said, something has happened," Tumpkin replied quickly. "Your eyebrows are getting thicker."

I snorted. "Well, if that's all curse forty-eight amounts to, I think Mother and Father should quit wasting time trying to break it. Who cares what my eyebrows look like?"

He didn't have an answer for that, so he told me about the latest book he was reading instead. I was feeling restless and impatient, but I knew Mother would be annoyed if I came home too early, so I made myself listen politely. At least I didn't have to say anything myself as long as Tumpkin was talking.

Tumpkin kept giving me speculative looks whenever he thought I wasn't looking. Finally I couldn't stand it any longer, and I left. I dawdled all the way home, and then when I arrived Mother and Father were talking and hardly even noticed me.

"... beyond the bounds of reason this time," Mother was saying as I came in. "Even you have to admit that."

"I'm sure the caliph has a reason," Father said in the stiff tone he uses when he knows he's wrong but can't say so.

"For a curse like this? We aren't talking about a petty inconvenience, Selim. This is a danger to everyone in the city. And there's no cure for lycanthropy."

"Caliph Arenschadd wouldn't endanger his people," Father said, even more stiffly than before.

"Maybe not if he thought about it first," Mother retorted. "But I don't think he's thought about this at all. Lycanthropy —"

"Imani!" Father said, spotting me at last. He shot Mother a look that was half warning, half relief. "When did you come in?"

"Just now," I said. I looked up at him. His eyebrows were getting thicker; they nearly met in the middle. Mother's were thicker, too. "What's lycanthropy?"

Mother and Father looked at each other. "You might as well explain, Selim," Mother said. "If we don't tell her, she'll just look it up in the dictionary."

Father sighed. "*Lycanthropy* means the assumption by human beings of the form and nature of wolves," he said, and looked down. "That's what the forty-eighth curse is, Imani. We've become werewolves."

"Well, I don't see what's so terrible about that," I said. I thought of my dream of running in the moonlight. "I think I'm going to like being a wolf."

They stared at me as if they'd never seen me before. Then Mother got a grim look on her face. "You'll find out soon enough," she said.

Mother was right. Two nights later I woke up well after midnight, feeling strange and tingly all over. I slipped out of bed and went out onto the balcony that overlooks our private garden. It was deep in shadow, because the moon was still on the other side of the house, rising. I could see the edge of the shadow creeping nearer as the moon rose, and I shivered in anticipation. I sat on the edge of the balcony, watching the line of moonlight come nearer, and waited.

The moon came over the domed roof of the house. I leaned into the silvery light and felt myself change. It was strange and exciting and scary all at once, though it didn't hurt at all. A moment later I stood on four paws and shook myself all over. Then I sat back and howled at the moon.

I heard answering howls from the corner of the house, and then two adult wolves came padding into sight below my window. Mother had turned into a slender, coal-black female; Father was dark gray and more solidly built. He had white hairs in his muzzle. I leaped down from the balcony to join them, and Mother cuffed me with her paw. I snarled, and she cuffed me again. Then Father made a sharp barking noise and we turned. Together we jumped over the garden wall and into the city streets.

The first thing I noticed was the smells. The whole city reeked of garbage and people and cooking spices and cats and perfumes. It was awful. I cringed and whined very softly. Mother bared her teeth in sympathy, and even Father coughed once or twice. Then we faded into the shadows and headed for the edge of town.

If it hadn't been for the smells, sneaking through the city like that would have been a lot of fun. As it was, I was glad we lived outside the city wall. Nobody saw us but a couple of dogs, and they ran when Father snarled at them. And then we passed the last of the houses and came out into the fields.

It was even better than my dream, to begin with. We ran and ran, and I could feel the wind in my fur and smell the fresh grass and the flowers and the little animals that had hidden as we approached. Now and then we'd stop and howl for the sheer joy of it. And all the while, the moonlight poured down around us in silver sheets.

Then we ran over the rabbit. Literally ran over it; the stupid thing was too scared to move when it heard us coming, and Father tripped over it. *Then* it ran, or rather, tried to. Mother caught it before it got very far. She trotted back with it while Father was picking himself up, and we split it between us.

The moon was getting low in the sky, and we began to feel a need to return home. I tried to fight it; I didn't want to go anywhere near that awful-smelling place again. But all I could do was whine and shuffle and edge closer. Mother cuffed me a couple of times because I wasn't going fast enough to suit her, and finally she nipped my tail. I yelped and gave up, and we ran back toward town.

As we passed the first house, we heard a baby crying inside. Mother and Father stopped and exchanged glances, just the way they'd done when they were people. Father looked up at the sky. The moon was close to setting; we had to get home. He growled and leaped forward, and Mother and I followed. A few minutes later, we reached our house and jumped over the garden wall.

Jumping back up to my balcony was harder than jumping down; I had to try twice, and I almost didn't make it in time. The moon set just as I scrabbled over the balcony rail, and I sprawled on the floor as a girl instead of a wolf. I sat up, remembering the wild run I'd just had.

Then I was sick to my stomach. Raw rabbit may be great when you're a wolf, but it's pretty disgusting to think about when you're a person.

I didn't get much sleep the rest of that night. I had too much to think about. I felt as if I'd been suckered: all those dreams about running in the moonlight, and not one about raw rabbit. I wondered how many other nasty surprises were in store for me. I thought of the way Mother and Father had looked at each other when they heard the baby cry. A cold shiver ran down my back, and I decided I didn't want to find out any more about being a werewolf. Then I remembered Mother's voice saying "There's no cure for lycanthropy," and I shivered again.

Mother and Father were late to breakfast the next morning, and when they came in they were arguing. "It's the only thing we can do," Mother insisted. "And after last night, we have to do *something*. If Imani hadn't slowed us down coming home, that baby might have been —"

"There has to be another alternative," Father interrupted. He sounded desperate.

"Suggest one," Mother said. "Bearing in mind that the moon still isn't completely full, so we'll have at least another three or four nights like the last one unless we solve this problem right away."

I looked up. "Mother! You've found a way to break the curse?"

"Not quite," Mother said. "But we've come up with something we hope will work just as well."

I looked from Mother to Father. "What are you going to do?"

Father sighed. "I'm going to apologize to Caliph Arenschadd," he said reluctantly.

Mother insisted that both of us go along with Father to apologize to the caliph. I'm not sure whether she was worried about Father's ability to be tactful or whether she thought Caliph Arenschadd would be more likely to relent if he were faced with all three of us at once, but she was very firm. So I had to spend all morning having my hair washed and perfumed and my hands painted, and putting on my best clothes. Then I had to wait while Mother and Father finished doing the same things. I had to sit practically without moving so I wouldn't muss my hair or tear my skirts or rub any of the paint off my hands. I hate court appearances.

When we got to court, we were ushered into the caliph's presence for a private audience. Father bowed and started in on the obligatory courtesies. I didn't bother listening; all that O-Radiant-Light-of-the-Universe stuff bores me. I looked around the audience chamber instead, and that was why I saw Tumpkin sneaking in at the back. I stiffened. *Nobody* is supposed to be at a private audience except the caliph, whoever he's seeing, and the deaf guards the caliph hires especially for private audiences. Tumpkin would be in real trouble if anyone else noticed him.

Father finished his apology. "Very nicely put," the caliph said, smiling. "Accepted. Was there anything else?"

"O Commander of Legions, the curse yet remains," Father said delicately. "That is, the forty-eighth curse of your renowned list of curses, which you in your great and no-doubt-justified anger cast over me and my wife and daughter."

"Of course it remains," the caliph said. He sounded a little testy. "When I curse someone, they stay cursed until they break it."

"O Fountain of Wisdom, you have said it better than your humble servant ever could," Father replied. "That is our difficulty precisely. For nowhere in all the scrolls and tomes and works of magic is written the cure for your forty-eighth curse, and so we have come to you to beg your mercy."

"You want me to lift the curse, is that it?" the caliph said, frowning. "I don't like the idea; it would set a bad precedent."

Father wiped his forehead with the end of his sleeve. "O Auspicious and Merciful Caliph, what is wrong with establishing that a man's punishment ends when he humbly acknowledges his error? Display your justice before the whole court, and remove this dreadful curse from me and mine."

"Well . . ."

"O Just and Sagacious Monarch, let me add my entreaties to my husband's," Mother said. She stepped forward and knelt gracefully in front of Caliph Arenschadd. "Have pity! Or if your heart is hardened against us, think of your subjects who huddle within their doors each night in fear while wolves prowl the streets. Think of them, and lift the curse."

"Get up, Mirza, get up," the caliph said. "You know that sort of thing makes me uncomfortable."

"O Caliph of Compassion, I cannot," Mother said, bowing her head so he couldn't see the annoyance on her face. "My limbs will not support both my body and the curse that weighs on me. Lift the curse, and I will stand."

"I can't," said the caliph.

"What?" said Mother and Father together.

"I didn't work out how to lift all the curses I made up," Caliph Arenschadd said self-consciously. "I didn't think I needed to."

"You mean you were too lazy to bother," Mother muttered. Father gave her a horrified look, but fortunately Caliph Arenschadd hadn't heard.

"O Powerful Sovereign, what then are we to do?" Father said.

"You'll just have to find a way to break it yourselves," Caliph Arenschadd said. He was trying to sound airy and unconcerned, but I could see that he was really embarrassed and worried. He wasn't much better than Father at pretending he was right when he knew he wasn't.

"But Commander of Legions, there *is* no cure for lycanthropy!" Father said.

"Not usually," Tumpkin said from behind the caliph. "But I think I know one that will work this time."

I shut my eyes, wondering what Caliph Arenschadd would do to Tumpkin for sneaking into a private audience and whether Tumpkin would be able to tell us how to break the curse before Caliph Arenschadd did it. Nothing happened, so after a moment I opened my eyes again. Mother, Father, and the caliph were all staring at Tumpkin, who looked pleased and proud and a little embarrassed by all the attention he was getting. Nobody seemed to be angry.

"My son, how can this be?" said Caliph Arenschadd. "You are still a beginner in wizardry. How can you do what my grand vizier" — he waved at Father — "his skilled and intelligent wife" — he gestured at Mother — "and myself cannot achieve?"

"It's not wizardry, Father," Tumpkin said. "It's just logic."

" *'Father'*?" I said indignantly. "You mean you're the *prince*? Why didn't you *tell* me?"

"Imani!" Mother said sharply. "Mind your manners! Pray forgive the impulsiveness of her youth, Your Highness."

"It's all right," Tumpkin said. "We've known each other for a long time."

"You seem to have many secrets I was not aware of, my son," said Caliph Arenschadd, but he couldn't keep from sounding proud instead of reproachful. "Therefore, tell us how you think to break this curse."

"It's just a theory," Tumpkin said. "But you told me once that your curses only work one at a time. If you cast another curse on the grand vizier, wouldn't that take the place of this one?"

Mother and Father and Caliph Arenschadd all stared at Tumpkin some more. I stared, too, thinking furiously. If Caliph Arenschadd put the next curse on Father, we'd be in the same situation we'd been in when Father got the forty-eighth curse, not knowing what the curse was or how to break it. Curse forty-nine could be just as bad as all this werewolf business. But if somebody *else* made the caliph mad . . .

"That's the stupidest thing I've ever heard," I said loudly.

Everyone turned to look at me. Mother and Father looked horrified; the caliph looked startled and unbelieving. Tumpkin grinned, and I knew he'd figured out what I was up to.

"Imani!" Mother said automatically.

"What was that you said, girl?" Caliph Arenschadd asked ominously.

I swallowed hard and said, "I said that that list of curses was a stupid idea. And it was even stupider not to figure out how to break them all. Stupid and lazy. And sticking in a werewolf curse was the stupidest thing of all. *Everybody* knows you can't break a werewolf curse, but I bet you didn't even think about it."

I paused for breath. The caliph was positively purple with rage; the minute I stopped talking, he pointed three fingers at me and said something that sounded like "Donny-skazle frampwit!"

I looked at Mother and Father. They were bright green.

I heaved a sigh of relief; I hadn't been quite sure

that Caliph Arenschadd would start over with the first curse on the list for me. I studied Mother and Father again, more closely. Their eyebrows were back to normal.

"It worked!" I said. I grinned at Tumpkin, then looked at Caliph Arenschadd. "Sorry about that, Your Majesty; I was just trying to make you mad."

"Imani . . ." Mother sounded as if she didn't know whether to laugh or scold me.

I shrugged. "Well, *somebody* had to do it. And I wasn't sure it would work right if the caliph wasn't really mad at somebody. 'Scuse me, Your Majesty."

"I believe I understand," the caliph said slowly. He looked from me to Tumpkin and back. "Just don't do it again, young woman. Audience concluded."

I went straight outside and walked backward around the palace three times, and that took care of being green. Then Mother and Father took me home and fussed over me. Father said I was quick-witted enough to make a fine diplomat, if I'd just learn a little tact; and he'd start my training tomorrow. Mother said that Father was a fine one to talk about tact, and she wasn't going to let him waste my abilities in politics. She was going to start teaching me sorcery that evening.

I left them arguing and went to see Tumpkin. He was waiting in the garden, just as I expected.

"You took a while getting here," he said.

"My parents wanted to argue," I explained. "Why didn't you tell me you were the prince?"

"I didn't think you'd believe me," Tumpkin said. "I don't look much like a prince, you know."

I snorted. "What's that got to do with anything?"

"It seems to matter a lot to some people," Tumpkin said, and neither of us said anything for a little.

"How did you figure out what to do about the curse?" I asked finally.

"I don't know," Tumpkin said. "I just thought about it a lot, after I found out it was a werewolf curse. I knew it was going to take something unusual to get rid of it, or your Mother and Father would have figured it out weeks ago."

"They'd never have thought of getting rid of one curse by replacing it with another," I said.

Tumpkin looked at me sidelong. "Was it very bad?" he asked.

"Some of it," I said shortly, thinking of the rabbit and the way the city streets smell to a wolf. Then I thought about running through the grass. "Some of it was wonderful."

Tumpkin didn't ask any more questions, and he never has. I think he understands, but he won't make me tell him about the details until I want to. That's why we're such good friends. I still call him Tumpkin, even though now I know he's really the prince.

A couple of weeks ago Caliph Arenschadd issued a new proclamation about punishing people who offend him. He's decided to turn them blue. The more times someone offends him, the bluer they get and the longer it lasts. Father talked him into it by pointing out that it's rather difficult to do most of the jobs in the palace with your eyelids stuck shut or three-foot fingernails, but no one will have to stop working just because he's blue. So no one else will ever work up to curse forty-eight, and we won't ever have to worry about were-wolves in town.

Which is a good thing, I suppose. But sometimes I still dream about moonlight and the wind in my fur as I run, and run, and run forever through endless, sweet-smelling grass.

Fairy Dust

At first Marina thought that
Jason had caught some sort of
odd bug. He came into her
family's backyard, where she
was weeding the vegetable
garden, and handed her an
old jam jar with nail holes
poked into its metal lid. She
sat back on her haunches to
look at his prize. The jar held
a twig that went almost all
the way from the bottom to its
top in two branched lengths.
Holding on to the twig was

a thin iridescent shape, about the length of a man's index finger.

"Don't look at it straight on," Jason told her as she held it up to her eyes.

Obediently Marina moved the jar to one side until she was looking at the bug from the corner of her eye. It remained a blur until suddenly—like the viewfinder of a camera finally snapping into focus—the iridescent shape shivered into clarity.

Marina's eyes went round and she almost dropped the jar. What she'd supposed was a bug looked for all the world like a tiny winged person: thin, angular limbs, dragonfly wings folded back along its spine. A short tunic of some sort of gossamer fabric covered its torso. The eyes were closed, the tiny head leaning against the side of the twig for support. Two needle-thin antennae protruded from a mass of miniature corkscrew curls the color of dark red sumac fruit.

"Where . . . where did you get it?" she breathed.

"At the bottom of the garden. Isn't it *something?*"

Reluctantly Marina took her gaze from the captured fairy to settle on Jason.

"You can't keep it."

"Why not?"

"It . . . it just wouldn't be right. It's something so magical"—so impossible, she added to herself—"that it would be wrong to keep it."

But it wasn't just the wrongness that bothered her. She was also thinking of what happened in her book of fairy tales whenever people came into contact with creatures from the Middle Kingdom: something always went terribly awry — especially when you actually meddled with the otherworld beings.

Jason looked uncomfortable. Two years junior to Marina, who was fourteen, he often seemed far younger to her. Her mother had told her once that girls matured much faster than boys. At times like this, it was far too obvious that she was right.

"I can't just let it go," he said.

"Jason!"

"I'll only keep it overnight," he compromised. "Okay? I'll let it go in the morning. I promise."

This still wasn't right, Marina thought, but it wasn't her fairy. Jason had caught it.

"You'd better keep that promise," she said.

But the next morning, the fairy was dead. All that remained in the bug jar was the branched twig with what looked like the husk of a long, thin dead beetle still attached to it. At the bottom of the jar lay a small mound of gray-brown dust and bits of things that might have been the fairy's limbs, so bone dry they were almost translucent.

And Jason was sick.

He lay in his bed, features washed out and thin as though he were the victim of a long debilitating disease that had plagued him for months. Marina almost couldn't recognize him, he was so changed.

"Get . . . get it . . . out of here," he managed to tell her before his mother shooed Marina out.

"Until the doctor comes by, we won't know if what he has is contagious or not," Jason's mother said. "So, better safe than sorry, right?"

She was trying to hide her worry but doing a poor job of it. And no wonder, Marina thought. Jason looked awful, as though he were about to die.

"You really can't stay," Jason's mother said.

Clutching the bug jar, Marina nodded mutely and fled for home.

An hour later, she was sitting at the picnic table in her own backyard, staring at the contents of the bug jar.

I warned him, she thought. I told him he shouldn't keep it. But he wouldn't listen. Jason rarely did. And now he was going to die of a fairy curse.

It wasn't fair. Discovering a fairy should have been a wonderful, magical moment, but Jason had reduced it to simple bug collecting.

She could imagine what her mother would say. She'd feel sorry for Jason, but then she'd add, "It doesn't surprise me at all. The only way people judge things anymore is by their material value — as something they can possess, important because they're the only one who has one, or as something that they can use to turn a profit."

It wasn't a whole lot different from the way her father had often complained about how people took all that was wonderful and beautiful about the earth and used it up and polluted it and ruined it so that by the time children Marina's age grew up, there'd hardly be anything left of it at all. Just memories of how it had once been. If that.

Marina often got the idea from things her mother had told her about her father that he and her mother'd had a lot of the same ideas about the important things in life. Which made it even harder for Marina to understand how her mother could have divorced him.

Marina had only one real memory of her father. She was twelve years old at the time and had forgotten her house key so she couldn't let herself in. Sitting on the front steps, waiting for her mother to get home from work, she'd watched an old derelict come shambling down the street. She'd seen people like that before, but only over by the public-housing project. Never in her own neighborhood. It was only when he got closer that she realized the man wasn't all that old, but his clothes were certainly threadbare. He looked as though he hadn't had a decent meal for a week.

He stopped at her walk and then came up its short length until he stood directly in front of her. He looked uncomfortable as he pulled a battered little book out of his pocket.

"I don't expect you know who I am," he said.

Marina shook her head. Surreptitiously, she glanced down the street, hoping to see her mother's car approaching. The man was making her nervous. Her mother's endless admonishment — "Don't talk to strangers" — rang clearly in her head. It probably went double for an old bum like this.

"Doesn't matter," the man said. "This is for you."

He handed her the book, which she took automatically before she remembered what her mother had also said about accepting gifts from strangers. But as soon as the book was in her hand, the man stepped back from her.

"Whatever you do," he said, "don't grow up to be like me. Make sure you're always considerate — not just to those who love you, but to everyone."

And then he walked away.

Marina looked at the book. On the cover were the simple words, *Fairy Tales*. She opened the book and there, in a neat script under the stamp that said Property of the Ottawa Public Library, had been written: "For my daughter Marina, in the hope that she will never consider herself too old to dream. Your loving father, Frank."

When Marina's mother talked about the man she had kicked out of her house the week after Marina was born, her voice was always affectionate until she got to one aspect of his personality. "He wanted to live on dreams," she'd tell Marina, her frustration plain. "He had no common sense, not a practical bone in his body."

"Did you love him, Mom?"

It seemed to Marina that love should be enough — wasn't it supposed to conquer all?

Her mother would nod. "But it was the wrong kind of love. It was the love that was only fire and heat; all it left behind was hurt."

Marina remembered her father's purported lack of practicality as she looked down at the book in her hand.

It figures, she thought. The first time I ever meet my father, all he does is give me a book he stole from the library. Worse, it was a book of fairy tales. Who reads this kind of stuff, anyway?

Having been brought up to do the right thing, Marina took the book back to the library that weekend, her apology for what had been written in it all ready to be offered. But the librarian only smiled.

"It was very conscientious of you to bring it back," she told Marina, "but this was sold in one of our book sales."

"You *sell* books?"

"Only when no one wants to borrow them from us anymore." She flipped to the inside back cover. "You see? It hadn't been taken out in twenty years."

No wonder. Who'd want to borrow a dumb old book of fairy tales?

But she was relieved that her father hadn't stolen it. And then, because it was all she had of him, she did read it. And was surprised to discover that she loved the stories. They weren't the simple fairy tales that she'd long ago decided she didn't much care for — the ones from the storybooks that her mother used to read to her. The language and plots of these were a lot more complicated than the ones her mother read. They were all twisty, like a rose garden gone wild, and full of strange turns that gave her little shivers.

She loved the pictures, too. Delicate watercolor reproductions that had been tipped in, rather than printed as part of the book, so that it was as though someone had glued the appropriate pictures into a photo album after first searching them out in flea markets or boxes of old prints in an antique shop. A few were missing, but she delighted in the ones that remained.

For some reason, she never told her mother about her brief meeting with her father or showed her the book. If asked, Marina might have said it was to spare her mother's feelings, but she knew that wasn't the real reason. The real reason was that it was all she had in terms of firsthand experience with her father — a brief conversation, a funny old book — and she wanted to keep it not so much secret as private.

Looking at the bug jar, Marina remembered the book again. Last night, her head filled with the premonitions she'd had about the wrongness of keeping the fairy jarred, she'd reread one story in it where a farmer named John Goodman captured a fairy in the woods. He took her to be his wife, but she pined and pined for her freedom until one day John came home and found her gone. All that remained of her was a little heap of old twigs and leaves and bits of moss, lying right there in the middle of the bed.

He took the changeling bits of what had been his wife, wrapped them up in his best cloak, and carried them into the forest, where he buried the bundle under an old oak tree. When he was done, he stood there with his head bowed and wept until he realized he was no longer alone. A strange old man had approached him on silent feet, his limbs all bent and gnarled, his hair like the fine hairs on a tree's roots, his cloak made of moss and leaves.

John knew right away that the old man was a fairy, too.

"Can't you bring her back?" he asked.

"I could," the old man told John, "but she wouldn't be the same."

"What do you mean?"

"She wouldn't be able to laugh or cry anymore, to be angry or content, or to feel anything at all. She would simply be—like a stone or a tree." Someone had underlined the next thing the old fairy man said; Marina thought it might have been her father. "Fairies are like thoughts. If you cage them, they will only wither and die."

It was the saddest story, not just because of what had happened to the poor fairy woman, but because of how terrible John had felt when he finally realized what he'd done. His love had blinded him until it was too late. Because he felt that he had made a mockery of it, he changed his surname to Sorrow.

After rereading the story, Marina had wanted to sneak into Jason's house and let the fairy go, but she'd been afraid of Jason's parents catching her in their house. What would she have said?

So she'd waited for the morning, until she, just like John Sorrow in the story, was too late as well.

Marina arose after a while and went into her house. She got the beautiful silk scarf that her mother had given her for her last birthday and brought it out to the picnic table. As carefully as she could, she took the twig from the jar and detached the beetlelike exoskeleton from it. She laid it in the center of her scarf, then poured the dust and bits and pieces from the bottom of the jar on top of it. Bundling it all up, she took it and a spade to the bottom of Jason's garden.

There was a cedar hedge there, separating Jason's garden from a strip of grassy land owned by the power company. It cut a swath through the subdivision to let the electrical towers march in a long, uninterrupted row. They looked, Marina often thought, just like giant metal stick people, connected only by their humming wires.

Marina buried her scarf under the hedge. It was hard work, spading through the dense roots of the cedars, but she felt she deserved worse than a little hard work for the part she'd played in the fairy's death. When she was finally done, she knelt in the grass beside the hedge.

"I'm so very sorry," she said. "Truly I am. And I know Jason meant no harm, so please let him get well again. If anything, I'm more to blame. He didn't know, but I did and I didn't do anything. I think maybe that's worse."

There was no reply, but she hadn't really expected one. She just went on, her voice sounding awkward and tight in her ears, but she knew she had to finish: "Please don't bring her back. It would be too horrible knowing that she was alive but could have no feelings."

She hesitated a moment, then added, "If I ever see someone doing something I know is wrong again, I promise I won't . . . I won't just stand by and watch."

Then her eyes filled with tears. Her chest got tight and her throat felt too constricted. She couldn't speak anymore, but there was nothing left to say.

When Jason did get better, he didn't remember having caught the fairy. He didn't remember it at all—or at least, so he said. But all the same, he put away his net and jars and never went hunting insects again.

Still, Marina remembered, and she kept her promise. The empty bug jar, sitting beside the book titled simply *Fairy Tales* on her bookshelf, served as a reminder in case she ever forgot.

WILL SHETTERLY

The Princess Who Kicked Butt

Once upon a time, not so very long ago, there was a land ruled with the very best intentions, if not the very best results, by the King Who Saw Both Sides of Every Question and the Queen Who Cared for Everyone. When their first child was born, the Fairy Who Was Good with Names arrived at the castle in a cloud of smoke and said, "Your daughter shall be known as the Princess Who Kicked Butt."

Before anyone could say

another word, the fairy sneezed twice and disappeared. A page ran to open a window, and when the smoke had cleared, the king said, "What did the fairy say?"

The queen frowned. "She said our daughter shall be called, ah, the Princess Who Read Books. I think."

"Hmm," said the king. "I'd rather hoped for the Princess Who Slew Dragons. But reading books is a sign of wisdom, isn't it? It's a fine title."

"I think she'll be happy with it," said the Queen.

So the Princess Who Kicked Butt was surrounded with books from her earliest days. She seemed happy to spend her time reading, when she wasn't riding or dancing or swimming or running around the kingdom talking with everyone about what they were doing and why they were doing it and how they might do it better. The king and the queen were delighted with their daughter, and only once did they express any doubt about her title.

The king said, "Have you noticed that she doesn't read very often?"

The queen shrugged. "The fairy didn't call her the Princess Who Read All the Time."

"That's true," said the king. And then he said, "Have you noticed that she reads fairy tales and adventure novels and almost nothing else?"

The queen shrugged again. "The fairy didn't call her the Princess Who Read Schoolbooks."

"That's true," said the King. "And if history remembers her as the Princess Who Read Silly Stories When She Had Nothing Better to Do, well, what does that matter if she's happy?"

One day when the princess was older than a girl but

younger than a woman, a page hurried into the throne room where the King Who Saw Both Sides of Every Question and the Queen Who Cared for Everyone were playing cards while they waited for some royal duties to do. The princess sat on a nearby windowseat, reading *The Count of Monte Cristo*.

"Your Majesties!" the page cried. "The Evil Enchanter of the Eastern Marshes demands to be admitted into your presence!"

"Well, then!" the king said. "Admit him immediately, lest he be angered by the delay."

"At once," said the page, and he turned on his heel to bring in the enchanter.

"Or perhaps," said the king (and the page turned back to face the king and queen so quickly that he almost fell over), "we should make the enchanter wait a few minutes, lest he think he can easily sway us to his whims."

"As you wish," said the page.

"Wait, wait," said the king. "Go at once to admit the enchanter. Not because we fear him, but because we would not have him think us rude."

"I go," said the page, turning to do so.

"But," said the king (and here the page did trip on the carpet as he turned, though he sprang quickly back to his feet), "if the enchanter is demanding to be admitted, that's rather rude, isn't it?"

The queen said, "For an evil enchanter, being rude might be the very best manners." Then she asked the page, "Have you had enough to eat? If you're dizzy from hunger, we should give you a raise."

"Thank you, Your Majesty," said the page. "But I

had a raise just last week, and I ate an excellent lunch."

The queen nodded. "Be sure you have milk with every meal. Milk builds strong bones."

"I don't think there's anything wrong with his bones, Mama," said the princess, who secretly liked the page.

The king smiled. "If the enchanter's being polite, we should be polite too, and if he's being rude, we'll look better by answering rudeness with civility. Don't dawdle, page. Admit him at once."

"At once," said the page, sprinting for the throne-room doors.

"Unless—" began the king. But the page slipped through the doors and closed them firmly behind him. The king barely had time to sigh before the doors opened again and the page returned. "Your Majesties, I give you the Evil Enchanter of the Eastern Marshes!"

The king smiled at the Evil Enchanter. "Welcome to our castle. Unless you'd rather not be."

"Oh, I'd rather be," said the Evil Enchanter. "Indeed, I feel most welcome to your lands, your people, and your treasure."

"Oh, good," said the king.

"I don't think so, dear," said the queen.

"What?" said the king, staring at the Evil Enchanter. "Do you mean that you feel welcome to keep my lands, people, and treasure?"

"I do," said the Evil Enchanter. "And I shall. My immediate marriage to your daughter followed by Your Majesties' abdication of the throne in my favor would be the simplest solution. Oh, and triple the taxes on the people. That would make a fine wedding present."

"Yes, I suppose so," said the king.

"Dear!" said the queen.

"— if I intended to permit that," said the king.

"I won't marry him," said the princess, thinking it best to let her father know her position on the matter as soon as possible.

"Of course not," said the king. "Arrest that man!"

The page looked around to see if there were any palace guards in the room. Since there were none, he said, "Sir? I'm afraid you're under arrest. Please step — "

The Evil Enchanter made a careless gesture. The page said, "I'm sorry to say I cannot arrest this man, Your Majesty. I cannot move my legs."

The king said, "Give my page the use of his legs! Immediately!"

"Certainly," said the Evil Enchanter. "When the princess consents to marry me."

Before the princess could speak, the queen turned to her. "Oh, my poor darling, how cruel of this enchanter! People will suffer, no matter how you choose!"

"It's kind of you to notice," said the Evil Enchanter.

"You're right, my dear," the king told the queen. "We shall decide, not she." He nodded at the princess. "And I say you shall marry this evil enchanter, lest he be provoked to further mischief."

"What?" said the princess, the Evil Enchanter, and the page simultaneously.

"But," said the king (and in different ways, the princess, the Evil Enchanter, and the page relaxed), "if we permit this, the enchanter's next demand will surely be even more unforgivable. Therefore, I say you shall not marry him."

"That's your last word?" said the Evil Enchanter.

"It is," said the king.

"Very well." The Evil Enchanter waved his arms once in a broad pass, and he, the king, and the queen disappeared in a cloud of smoke, just as the king said, "Unless—"

The princess and the page stared at the places where the three people had been. The page carefully lifted each of his feet, just to be sure that he could, then ran to open a window. When he quit coughing, he said, "What shall we do, Your Highness?"

"Why, I'll rescue them, of course," said the princess.

"I'll accompany you!" said the page.

The princess said, "Don't be silly. Someone has to run the country while I'm gone." Before the page could reply, the princess strode from the throne room into the inner waiting room, and then into the outer waiting room, and then into the long hall, and then into the entryway, and then into the courtyard, and finally into the royal stables.

The royal hostler bowed as she said, "I need a horse."

"Of course." He gestured toward a lean midnight-black mare. "This is Arrives Yesterday, the fastest horse in the land."

"Won't do," said the princess.

"Of course not," said the royal hostler, stepping to the next stall, which held a broad-shouldered golden stallion. "This is Carries All, the sturdiest horse in the land."

"Won't do," said the Princess. She stepped to the

next stall, which held a wiry horse with black-and-white splotches on its gray hide. "And this?"

The hostler swallowed and said, "This is Hates Everything, the angriest horse in the land."

"Perfect," said the princess. And before the hostler could say another word, she saddled Hates Everything and rode out from the palace.

The moment they passed through the palace gates, Hates Everything tried every trick that every horse has ever tried to escape from its rider, and then Hates Everything invented seventeen new tricks, each cleverer than the one before. But the princess held onto Hates Everything's back when he bucked, and she lifted her right leg out of the way when Hates Everything scraped his right side against the wall of the palace, and she lifted her left leg out of the way when Hates Everything scraped his left side against a tree. She ducked when Hates Everything ran under a low branch. She jumped off when Hates Everything flipped head over heels onto his back, and then she jumped right back into the saddle when he stood up again. Finally Hates Everything stood perfectly still in the middle of the road, snorting steam and glaring angrily from side to side.

Two palace guards stood by the gate, watching helplessly. One whispered to the other, "Did the fairy really call her the Princess Who Read Books?"

"Maybe she read a book about riding," said the other guard.

"You're just wasting time," the princess told Hates Everything. "You're not going to get rid of me."

Hates Everything jumped straight up in the air, did a triple somersault, and landed on his feet with the princess still on his back. "You see?" said the princess. "When you carry me to the palace of the Evil Enchanter of the Eastern Marshes, I will set you free."

Hates Everything turned his head to look back at her.

The princess said, "Don't you hate wasting time?"

Hates Everything raced eastward toward the marshes and the palace of the Evil Enchanter.

When they came to a raging river where the bridge had been swept away, Hates Everything halted and reared up on his hind legs. The princess clung to his back and whispered, "Don't you hate being stuck on this side?" Hates Everything plunged into the fierce currents and swam, carrying the princess across the water.

When they came to a landslide that blocked the road, Hates Everything halted and reared up on his hind legs. The princess studied the mountain of rocks and boulders before them. Then she whispered, "Don't you hate stopping when you're almost at your destination?" Hates Everything charged forward, bounding from boulder to boulder, carrying the princess up and over the landslide.

When they came to a pack of gray wolves that growled as they paced back and forth across the road, Hates Everything reared up on his hind legs and turned to gallop away. The princess whispered, "Don't you hate people who get in your way?" Hates Everything bolted forward, and the leader of the wolves had to jump aside lest he be trampled by Hates Everything's hooves.

They came at last to the Evil Enchanter's castle in the Eastern Marshes. A goblin the color of granite stood in front of the Evil Enchanter's gates. He called, "Have you come to marry my master?"

"No," said the princess.

"Then I cannot let you pass," said the goblin. A long sword appeared in his hands.

"Your fly's open," said the princess.

"Oh!" said the goblin, dropping the sword and turning away to button up its trousers. Then it turned back. "Wait a minute! I'm a goblin! I don't wear clothes!"

But the princess and Hates Everything had already ridden past the goblin and into the Evil Enchanter's courtyard. "Mama! Papa!" called the princess. "I've come to rescue you!"

The Evil Enchanter appeared in a cloud of smoke. He waved his arms to fan away the fumes, and when he quit coughing, he said, "You've come to rescue no one. Now that you're here, you shall marry me." He waved his arms once, and a priest appeared in a cloud of smoke. After everyone quit coughing, he turned to the priest and said, "Marry me!"

The priest said, "But I don't know you."

"No, no, no!" said the Evil Enchanter. "Marry me to the princess!"

"Oh," said the priest. "That's different."

The princess whispered to Hates Everything, "When we've defeated the enchanter, you'll be free. Don't you hate — "

But Hates Everything had already lunged forward and begun to chase the Evil Enchanter around the courtyard.

"Wait! Stop!" cried the Evil Enchanter. "I can't make a spell if I can't stop to think!"

"That's the idea," said the princess.

"Stop this crazy horse, please!"

"Then free my parents and quit trying to marry me and promise not to bother anyone ever again."

"What!" said the Evil Enchanter in outrage, and then "Ow!" said the Evil Enchanter in pain as Hates Everything nipped his buttocks. "It's a deal!"

"On your word of honor as an evil enchanter!"

"Yes! Yes!"

"Very well." The princess leaped down from the saddle. "Hates Everything, you're free to go."

Hates Everything seemed as if he hated having to stop chasing the Evil Enchanter (and he probably did), but he came to the princess and looked at her as if maybe he didn't hate her as much as he hated everything else. The princess removed his saddle and gave him a hug, and he let her do that, even though he clearly hated it. Then he charged away from the enchanter's palace as if he didn't hate anything at all.

The Evil Enchanter said, "You didn't really beat me. The horse beat me."

The princess yelled, "Goblin!"

The goblin ran into the courtyard. "Hey, it's you! Couldn't you tell that I wasn't wearing any clothes? So how could my fly be open, huh?"

Instead of answering that, the princess said, "I'll double your salary if you'll cut off the enchanter's head."

"Good deal!" said the goblin, and his long sword appeared in his hands.

"Wait!" said the Evil Enchanter. "Okay, okay. You beat me fair and square."

"Don't cut off his head," said the princess.

"Darn," said the goblin.

"You can still come and work at our palace," said the princess.

"Good deal," said the goblin.

The Formerly Evil Enchanter waved his arms, and the king, the queen, the goblin, the enchanter, the priest, and the princess all appeared in the throne room where the page was assembling the country's generals to go rescue their missing royal family. The page ran to open a window, and when everyone had stopped coughing, the princess said, "Papa? See how well the page managed things while we were gone? Don't you think you should make him a prince and engage him to your daughter?"

"I hadn't—" said the king, but the queen nudged him with her elbow, and he said, "Oh, right. That's exactly what I was planning to do. If that's all right with you, young man."

The page smiled shyly at the princess, then said, "Yes, Your Majesty, that's very much all right with me."

The Formerly Evil Enchanter said, "What about me?"

The king said, "You can't be engaged to my daughter, too."

The princess said, "That's not what he meant. He meant it gets awfully lonely on the Eastern Marshes." She cupped her hands and yelled, "Fairy Who's Good with Names! Am I really the Princess Who Read Books?"

The Fairy Who Was Good with Names appeared in a cloud of smoke. When everyone had quit coughing, the fairy said, "Indeed not! You're the Princess Who Kicked Butt."

"That's more like it," said the princess.

"Oh, my," said the queen.

"Hey," said the Formerly Evil Enchanter to the Fairy Who Was Good with Names. "Nice smoke!"

And then the priest, who still didn't know what was going on but who knew a good opportunity when it presented itself, gave everyone a business card that said, in large print, Marriages Are Our Favorite Business.

And they all lived happily ever after.

BETTY LEVIN

The Sea Giants

At the water's edge, an old woman gropes for a handhold on a beached canoe. Then, stiff and slow, she stoops down until her other hand brushes the shallows. The People gather around her.

"Why is Great-Grandmother doing that?" asks one of the children.

"To see if the whales come."

"But how can she? She is blind."

The child is hushed.

The old woman lets her hand float. The water surges, then recedes. She squats, waiting. A rim of foam seethes at her ankles. Her fingers rake the water; they dig beneath the surface.

"Well, Mother," asks one of the People, "what do you hear?"

The old woman does not answer, but the child speaks out. "Great-Grandmother is deaf. How can she hear the whales?"

"With her fingers," someone explains. "She listens with her fingers."

The old woman closes her sightless eyes. She tilts her head. Her fingers plow deep furrows in the sea.

One of the older men reminds the People of times gone by when the great whales, longing for the land, beached themselves to die.

But the whales the old woman hears now are far from land. They are past the islands, beyond the fog bank.

At last she nods. She is helped to straighten up. She has heard the song of the whales. "It goes like this," she tells the People, and she hums a breathy tune.

Standing before her, the child shouts a question: "What do you sing?"

"I sing the truth," she answers. "These are the words of it. Listen."

Everyone draws close. Some already know the words. Others will hear them for the first time. But even the child knows how they will begin: *In the Old Time . . .*

In the Old Time the trees and rivers and rocks could

45

change and be changed. They held power. They could speak and they could sing.

In the Land Next to Sunrise a large family of small People lived beside the sea. Their nearest neighbors were so far away that they were someone else's neighbors instead. The mother and father struggled to feed their children, but life was hard. The fish they caught were no bigger than herring, no meatier than eels. When the father hunted in the woods, he seldom returned with more than the tiniest forest creatures hanging from his belt — shrews and mice, chipmunks and jays. When the mother and her children dug roots and picked gooseberries and blueberries and raspberries on the grassy headland above the sea, there was seldom more than a taste for each of them, and sometimes the mother had nothing for herself but blue and red stains on her fingers.

"If only things would change," grumbled the husband. If only he were taller and fatter and stronger and faster. If he were a whale of a man, he would bring down moose and bear. He would be envied for his hunting ground. He would be a very great chief.

One early morning as the father and mother carried their canoe into the shallows, the father said, "Maybe this will be the day of our changing. Maybe we will hook so great a fish that it will feed us all winter." The wife said that if such a fish could be found, it would no doubt eat them instead. She pointed to a small fir tree growing out of a crevice in the sea cliff. If that tree could cling to life on the rock and bear the wind and salt spray, then their family could manage on herrings and eels.

46

When the mother and father had paddled far from land, a dense fog closed around them. The coastline vanished. The black ledges fringed with white foam turned to lumpy gray waves. The mother and father could not tell which way to go or where the current carried them. The fog dripped down their faces and trickled inside their sleeves. They felt dismal and helpless.

They drifted awhile, then paddled, then drifted once more. Voices came floating through the fog. The People heard paddles stroking the sea. Suddenly an enormous shape loomed up beside them. It might have been a sea rock the size of a mountain. But as they peered through the gloom, they saw that it was a huge canoe with giants in it. One of these called them Little Brother and Little Sister.

When he asked where they were heading, they had to admit that they were lost in the fog.

The speaker told them that his father, who was a chief, would welcome them into his camp. The People were fearful and amazed, but the giant spoke so gently that they believed he meant no harm. He and his companions placed their paddles under the couple's canoe and lifted it into their own as easily as if it were a wood chip. The giants handed around the canoe with its tiny man and woman the way children show each other a baby squirrel cowering in their hands.

After a while the enormous canoe ran up onto a beach. The People caught a glimpse of steep mountains, but at the next glance saw that those mountains were immense wigwams.

The chief came striding to greet them. "What have

you there?" he asked his son as he gazed down at the man and woman. "Where did you find this little brother and sister?"

"In the fog, my father," the giant responded, "in the sea." He picked up the canoe with the mother and father still seated in it. Taking care not to tip them out, he carried them into his father's wigwam.

After the canoe was set down and the People clambered out of it, it was set up high among the dried weeds and smoked meats, beyond the People's reach.

A great meal was set before them. The chief reminded the other giants that these little folk could not eat so much. He spoke in a whisper so that the man and woman would not be alarmed. Even so, his voice sounded to them like the creaking of the tallest trees in their hunting ground.

Each day the man and woman ate as much as they could. The giants went hunting and returned with moose and bear and caribou hanging from their belts. The man gasped at the sight. But the woman maintained that on the giants those animals were as mice and shrews and jays on the People. And it was soon clear that the giants required many moose and bear and caribou to satisfy their hunger. Yet they shared all they had.

"So," remarked the woman, "these sea giants may be taller and fatter and stronger and faster, but they do not seem so much better off than we are."

Her husband made no answer.

Each day the giants found some new way to show the small folk how greatly they cared about them. So when the chief, who could see farther than anyone else, declared that in three days' time they would be attacked, he persuaded the People to cover their ears and bind up their heads. They were rolled in so many skins that they looked like cocoons. Even so, the war cries nearly deafened them.

When the screams died out and the man and woman were unwrapped, they found the chief as serene as ever. Although many of his sons were sorely wounded, they had all survived. The enemy had fled.

Life returned to what it had been among these gentle sea giants. Then one evening the chief stared long into the fire and saw that in three days' time the enemy would raid his peaceful camp once more.

This time the People did not need to be persuaded to hide from the deafening war cries. They let the giants bind up their heads and bundle them into so many skins that they had to be put to bed like dolls.

For all that, the terrible din pierced the baffle of skins. The People shook and quaked until the battle din faded and they were unbound. They saw that giants had been stuck with pine trees and oaks and hemlocks, which they had to pluck from each other the way the People removed porcupine quills embedded in their own flesh. And they saw the chief's youngest son fall to the ground in his father's doorway. He could not rise again; he did not stir.

The chief ordered his sons to carry their brother to the shore. The People followed. When the sea giants laid their brother at the water's edge, the tide came swiftly to carry him out to sea. The People heard the sound of a great breath, a *whoosh,* and something huge rolled slowly out beyond the shallows. Spray leaped up to the sky. As the People gazed in wonderment, a great whale surfaced and then vanished beneath the water.

Some days later the chief asked the People if they had grown weary of this quiet life. They replied that they were content, but that they worried about their own children at home. The chief understood and promised to send them on their way the very next morning. Reaching up to the top of his wigwam, he brought down their canoe. His sons filled it with the finest furs and meat.

At daybreak everyone went down to the shore. The canoe was held for the People. When they were seated, the chief called a small gray dog and placed it in the middle of the canoe. He said the dog would show them the way home. But only the father, who sat in the stern, could see that the little dog pointed out to sea.

The sea giants shoved the canoe off. The chief called out to the People, asking them to remember him and his sons. In seven years' time, he declared, the man and the woman would be reminded of him. Knowing how truly he had foretold the battles, they had no reason to doubt him. But seven years is a long time, and their thoughts were on their home and their children.

They paddled and paddled. The fog came, but the little gray dog kept them on course and the water stayed smooth. When at last they reached their homeland, the little dog leaped from the canoe and ran to greet the children, who scrambled down the rocks to reach their mother and father. The dog was everywhere, licking every hand and face. Then, tail wagging, it turned to the mother and father, covering their eyes and their ears with its quick, moist tongue. After that it raced across the water. The children were amazed to see the dog cavorting on the surface of the sea. But the mother and father had seen so many strange and wonderful things that they were beyond marveling.

"Look!" cried their youngest child, pointing out to sea.

Where they looked, they saw nothing.

"Look!" the child told them. "There is the dog."

Just then the creature leaped free of the waves, and they could see it was a gray porpoise. It rose again and again in great looping curves as it raced away toward the horizon.

The People, young and old, came together to feast on all that the mother and father had brought home with them. After that they went back to their hunting and fishing and berrying.

But everything was changed. Expecting eels, the father caught salmon. Hoping for a few goslings, he had instead the fattest geese. Where once he had struggled to find enough mice and chipmunks to feed his hungry children, now there was enough game for all. And the berries would not ripen until the mother and her children cupped their hands beneath them. Then the berries dropped, plump and juicy and scarcely bruised by the eager fingers plucking them.

So the family lived, one season joining the next, until the seventh summer came. The light stayed long in the evenings and turned the sea a milky gray. For the father the brief nights were dream-filled, and he thought himself back in the land of the sea giants. But on the night before the longest day, he dreamed that he stood in front of his own wigwam. As he looked out over the water, a whale came swimming as close to land as it could. It sang a sweet, wild song.

When the father awoke, he wondered whether some of the power of the sea giants had come inside him. His wife just shook her head. "It is enough to be one of the People," she pleaded. "You do not need to be a whale of a man. It is enough to hold firm to our land as the fir tree on the cliff clings to the rock." The husband glanced at the little tree. How stunted it looked, bent from years of buffeting sea winds.

That day he and his wife caught sight of a shark swimming back and forth quite close to shore. Every fish and bird fled from it. The People were uneasy until the shark swam out of sight. They cast anxious glances seaward, imagining that they glimpsed it there, and there. But what they saw turned out to be the little gray dog trotting toward them over the water. The dog was as gleeful as before, dancing all around them. Yet it gazed up at the father, until the mother told him that the dog was waiting for him to speak.

So the father said, "In a while I will visit your master. When I am ready, I myself will find the way."

At once the little dog licked his hands and eyes and ears. Then it turned tail and trotted out over the water. Where it finally seemed to sink beneath the waves, in its place a gray porpoise leaped.

The father was troubled. Sometimes, when the mother urged him to stay at home with his family, that was all he wanted. But every time he could feel the warm, moist tongue of the little dog on his hands and eyes and ears, he yearned to be off. And when he heard again the sweet, wild song of the whale, he could scarcely keep from grabbing his paddle and shoving off into the water.

On the day he chose to leave his home for the land of the sea giants, the mother tried to hold the canoe back from the sea. Then the tide rose and lifted the canoe free and carried him away.

When the fog closed in around him, he found that he could see what he must and hear what was needed to keep from running his canoe onto the treacherous ledges. He paddled on until at last he broke through the fog and saw the immense wigwams rising above the beach, the great canoe drawn up from the water's edge.

The chief came slowly to welcome him. Although still tremendous, he was stooped with age and sorrow. All his sons had died at the end of the longest day, just after a great shark had been seen.

"Since then," the chief declared, "I have waited for you to come and take my power and my place, so that I can be with them once more. I have waited for you to be ready for the Change, so that I may join my sons in our own true home."

The chief brought clothes belonging to his sons and said the man must put them on. It was like asking him to clothe himself with a wigwam made from the bark of as many trees as covered a mountainside. The smallest fold in the fabric was deep as a river gorge.

The man felt a chill, for the clothing covered him in darkness and shut out all daylight. He thought of his wife and children. Would any of them find their way through the fog to come to him?

The old chief stood silently, waiting for the Change.

The man looked up into the immense space between his naked body and the covering so far beyond his reach. Shivering, he closed his eyes. He could feel the garments close around him until at last they fit. The Change had come into him.

Now he had all he had longed for, great size and strength and the power to see through the fog of time.

He had to learn the gentle ways of the chief and his sons, for the time would come when he too might hold other lives in his powerful hands — his own children's, perhaps, and strangers' as well.

But not his wife's. She was not to join him in this place. She would not become a sea giant, not ever. She would remain in the Land Next to Sunrise, growing smaller and bent like the little fir tree. He would live for a long time parted from her and from the land itself, until the sea called him for the last time.

The old woman falls silent. No one speaks or moves. The sea heaves itself onto the low-lying rocks. It mutters and sighs; it swallows the words of the whale song.

On the cliff above the gathering, the fir tree creaks. Its roots slide from the crevice. Nestled in the loosened soil, a seedling fir strikes new hairy tendrils straight down. For a while the rock will shelter it so that it can grow straight toward the light. After that it must stand up to the wind, the fog, the sea.

J O Y   O E S T R E I C H E R

Efrum's Marbles

Efrum was not a typical giant. At thirty-three, he looked like a child of six — except that he was bigger than any elf or other folk, of course.

Accordingly, he spent his time playing bagball, chase-the-duck, and marbles. He liked marbles a lot.

He kept his marble collection in a leather sack. His favorite among the little glass and stone balls was not made of glass or stone at all. His playmates, the children of other giants, sometimes screeched that it was a steelie, and unfair. But it wasn't a steelie either. In fact, it looked like an eyeball. As you might imagine, it was the object of much speculation.

Efrum wrapped it in silk and placed it carefully at the bottom of his sack. If he was winning, he never took it out. If he was losing and reached into his sack and felt only the silk wrapping, he would get a sick feeling in his stomach. His fingers would pull that last marble out, and while he unwrapped it the giant children would groan and complain, and Efrum would feel ill.

What if he lost it? It was the finest shooting marble that anyone had seen. Efrum didn't use it most of the time, because it was important to him to win without it. But if it made the difference between having some marbles and having no marbles, Efrum would pull it out and shoot with it, and he would win a few pieces to put back into the sack so the eye did not rest there alone. Each time he used it, his belly would clench. Sick with fear, he would risk his prize.

The marble-playing field was a place of fine, soft dirt that the giant children would sweep with the edges of their big brown hands until the circle was smooth gray dust. They avoided the few trees scattered over the field because shadows could make the play deceptive, especially if there was a breeze and the leaves were moving.

Efrum hated to put his marble down in the dirt. At the end of play, the gleaming blue-and-silver surface would bear a grimy film, and Efrum would have to wipe it off on his shirt, and it would always look at him before he could wrap it in its silk.

The other giants would pretend not to look at it, but they ended up staring just the same. No one could decide if Efrum's marble was really a dragon's eye or a wizard's. It was deadly accurate. It seemed to help Efrum aim and shoot, and it often captured more in a single shot than an ordinary marble would. Dragons, of course, are well known for their poor eyesight, but nevertheless it looked like a dragon's eye. A wizard's would have been yellowy, and how would a wizard have lost his eye in the first place?

You might think that the other children would have banned Efrum from their games, since once he pulled out the eye, he was sure to clear the circle. But giants are both smarter and dumber than other folks. They figured that if he wasn't playing marbles Efrum would be doing something else. It might be something *worse* than winning all their marbles, something they would like even less. They would think of things someone might do with a magic eye, and they would shudder. They'd rather have him on his knees in the dirt, where at least they knew what to expect.

Besides, there were a few older players who could sometimes win in spite of the eye. Though this happened exceedingly rarely, its very rarity made it a goal fervently desired. The big winner would walk away with everything on the field, and Efrum would have to reach into his sack, where he'd kept the eye in reserve. He'd use the eye against other kids to win back playing stock. Or he'd have to take time out to trade for new marbles, so he was out of play awhile.

Maybe someday someone would win the eye as well.

There was a girl giant named Brinda, attractive as giants go, who was an especially good player. She wore her long green hair in a pair of raggedy braids that she tucked into her shirt when she played (because otherwise they'd swing forward and mess up her shot).

Now, even though Efrum was kind of small and looked like a six-year-old, he was really thirty-three, you'll recall—which is a lot like being fifteen in humans, or about seventeen among the dwarven folk (though with elves, it's equivalent to being a toddler in a sodden breechclout). So Efrum was drawn to Brinda, as you might have guessed, in a way he did not understand. In fact, he kind of wanted her to win, because he thought that might make her like him better, even though he was not at all sure why he wanted her to like him in the first place. You can see that Efrum would find this confusing.

So maybe he played a little less well than he might have whenever she was in the game. Not that he'd ever let her take the eye, but he wanted her to be . . . well, *happy*.

Things came to a turning point, as such things do.

Brinda won and won, until Efrum lost all his marbles. He was down to the eye, and Brinda was holding out her hand for that, too. She'd used her fine leopard-agate shooter to hit Efrum's last marble, a pale blue alley, and knock it from the circle. But on its way out, the alley had ricocheted off Brinda's own black cat's-eye, then struck in turn *all* the remaining marbles in the ring, knocking them out before it, itself, spun from the circle. Brinda's aggie shooter rolled to a stop in the perfect center of the playing ring.

By giant rules, this meant each player in the game owed Brinda a shooter, in addition to the marbles she'd captured from the ring.

Of course, Efrum had only the eye.

Brinda held out her hand.

Efrum looked at her and clutched his flattened leather marble sack against his chest. Just the silk-wrapped eye remained, a small-seeming lump at the bottom. He wanted her to like him, but this was going too far.

Listen, Efrum. Think about this, Brinda said. When did you get the eye?

Won it when I was six, Efrum said.

Uh huh. From that dweeb dwarf named Miske.

Yeah.

Well, do ya know what *Miske* means in dwarvish?

Nope.

It means *baby*. Or *little one*.

Dwarf folk are always little ones. Efrum grinned.

But Miske was littler than most, she said, and now he's normal. For a dwarf. Why was that, Efrum? And *when did you stop growing?*

Being both smarter and dumber than human folk, it took Efrum but a moment to work it out. Shoot, he said. Do you think it could be the eye? But then, I *surely* don't want to give it to you, Brinda.

I have the perfect place for it, she said. Besides, I won it fair and circle.

Well, she had, so Efrum sighed and handed it over.

Efrum could feel himself sort of s-t-r-e-t-c-h. And he felt hungry, too.

Brinda unwrapped the eye from the silk. She held it up to the light so everyone could see it one last time.

Then she gave Efrum a big grin and put the eye carefully into the bottomless pocket her uncle had given her. It rested on a display rack in one of the lost dimensions the pocket could access.

It's staring at you now, of course.

TAPPAN KING

"Come Hither"

Not long ago, in a city by the sea, lived a girl with a mischievous nose. Her name was Margaret Mehitable McGillicuddy Malone, though everyone called her Meg. Mostly she was a well-behaved child, but her nose had a way of getting her into trouble when she wasn't watching it.

Part of the problem was that Meg was a middle child. The three Malone girls had been born one right after another, a year and a day apart, and Meg got stuck in the middle. Maureen was the Eldest, so she got to do everything first and was praised for being grown up and capable and helpful (though she was mostly a smug little goody-two-shoes). Melody was the Baby, so she had an even better deal. She always got off easy and was fussed over for being cute and charming and helpless (though she was mostly a nasty little brat).

But Meg was just the Middle One. The good jobs had all been taken, and there wasn't much left for her besides mischief. She was bright, and brash, and easily bored, and the only way she ever got noticed was by getting into trouble.

Being the middle child bothered Meg most each year when birthdays came around, one day after another. Mr. and Mrs. Malone had decided long ago to give each girl her own birthday party, just to keep the peace. Maureen's was always the most exciting, because it came first. And Melody's birthday was always special, because it was the last.

But there was never anything interesting for Meg's birthday. It was always just stuck in the middle. Meg sometimes wished that she'd been born the Eldest, or the Baby, so that Mo or Mel could see how it felt to be stuck in the middle for a change.

This year was the worst of all. Tomorrow Meg was going to turn ten, which should have been a very special birthday indeed. But Maureen was having her eleventh birthday party today, and Melody would have her ninth birthday party two days later, and nobody seemed to be doing much of anything about Meg's. In fact, Meg's nose had been so mischievous lately that her parents had hinted there would be no birthday presents at all for her this year if she kept it up. So the morning of Maureen's party, Meg found herself following her nose into the big hall closet where her parents always hid the birthday presents, just to make sure they hadn't forgotten her completely.

When no one was looking, Meg dragged the big stepstool from the kitchen into the closet, shut the door, and turned on the light, then climbed up the steps and stretched up on tiptoe, poking through the pile of brightly wrapped packages perched on the tip-top shelf to see if there was one with her name on it.

But while she was teetering on the top of the stepstool, the packages slipped from her grip and fell with a crash, and a moment later Meg came tumbling after them. The next thing she knew, she was sprawled on the floor amid the pile of presents with her mother and father glaring down at her, Mo sneering over one shoulder, and Mel grinning gleefully over another.

So Meg missed Mo's party and got sent to her room — or rather, the room she shared with her sisters — with a warning that if she didn't behave herself from now on she'd miss her own birthday party as well. At first she amused herself by reading books and playing games. But then she heard laughter from the party downstairs, and she began to feel sad, and then angry, and then bored, and she began to poke her nose into her sisters' things.

There was nothing interesting in Mel's toy box but an old dead frog, and the dresser drawer where Mo kept her diary was locked. But over in the corner, Meg noticed the draped shape of Maureen's computer, and her nose began to twitch.

Maureen had gotten the computer a year ago, on *her* tenth birthday, when she'd brought home a straight-A report card. (Except for gym. Mo was a spaz in gym.) Their parents had made it clear to Meg and Mel that they were not to use it without Maureen's permission. Sometimes Mo let Meg and Mel use it to play games, or write stories, or compose papers for class, but the rest of the time it was strictly off-limits.

Tonight, though, Meg didn't care. She whipped the cover off the computer and pressed the On switch. It made a soft *bong* sound, and when the screen lit up Meg began nosing around in Maureen's computer's files. Most were too boring for words. There was some homework, a catalog of Maureen's book collection, and some stupid pictures Mo had drawn of castles and horses and girls with long eyelashes. The only interesting thing was a half-written gooey love story in which a lonely only child named Maureen was carried off by a handsome gypsy named Heathcliff. (Meg wondered why her sister named her hero after a cartoon cat.)

Finally Meg found a folder with a picture of a telephone on it and she double-clicked it, just to see what would happen. The screen filled with a long list of telephone numbers. Meg knew she wasn't supposed to use the telephone, but her parents hadn't said anything about using a computer to make calls. So Meg closed her eyes, moved the mouse around in a circle, and double-clicked.

When she opened her eyes again, the computer had started to make a sound like a tiny telephone was dialing, and then it gave a loud, high-pitched squeal. Meg jumped, wondering if she'd been heard. But no one seemed to have noticed. Then Meg heard a quick beeping sound and saw words appear on the screen in front of her.

What subject would you like to find?

Meg started to type the word "fun," but in the middle, her nose sneezed, and her fingers fumbled, and it came out "elf" instead. She tried to erase it, but the word had already been sent, and these words appeared on the screen:

One moment, please. Searching . . .

A moment later, the screen turned bright green. For a moment, Meg was worried that she'd broken it, but then gleaming green-gold letters began to trace their way across the screen. At first she couldn't make them out, but the longer she looked at them, the clearer they became.

Come Hither!

Meg stared at the screen. She thought she remembered those words from an old poem her father used to read to her when she was very young. If she remembered right, they were an old-fashioned way of saying *Come here*. She guessed this must be some sort of game.

"Where?" she typed.

Her words vanished, and a moment later new ones appeared:

> Under the Hill,
> Over the Sea,
> Here by the spreading
> Green Wood Tree:
>
> Come Hither!

Meg wasn't bored anymore. "How?" she typed, waiting breathlessly for a response.

A moment later, the words changed:

> Who longs to come
> And play with me
> Must choose to follow
> Willingly:
>
> Come Hither!

Meg was excited. Her hands flew over the keyboard. "I'm willing," she typed. "What do I have to do?"

> Abandon Hope
> And banish Fear;
> Type 'Yes' three times
> And 'Enter' here:
>
> Come Hither!

Meg grinned. This was better than any stupid old

birthday party! "Yes," she typed. "Yes," and once again, "Yes!"

The green screen began to blur, and Meg found herself drawn into it. The flurry of colored dots began to look like falling leaves and swirling snowflakes, dancing limbs and grinning faces. Slowly words began to form again. As they appeared, Meg found the images coming to life, changing from letters to pictures in her mind's eye.

> You are standing all alone in a deep wood,
> under the shade of a tall oak tree.
> At once, a young man dressed all in green
> appears from behind a tree and speaks:
>
> "There you are! Took you long enough!"

The last line was in a different style, somehow sprightly and more playful. Meg could almost hear the voice behind the words.

"What did you say?" Meg typed back.

The reply came swiftly. "I said, it took you long enough to get here."

"To get where?"

"Why, here, the Green Wood. Isn't it beautiful?"

"How would I know?" Meg replied. "I can't see anything but words on a screen."

"Of course you can! Why, look over to your left, just above your head. There's a boggle sitting on that tree limb, just staring at you! Say 'Halloo' to the young lady, Boggle!"

In the upper left part of the screen, the word

"HALLOOOOO!" suddenly appeared, in squat, ugly letters the color of old moss.

"You see! There he is, just as plain as the nose on your face!"

"So you say," Meg answered, huffily, since she'd always been rather self-conscious about her nose. "I don't see why I should take your word for it. Who are you, anyway?"

Suddenly the screen was filled with laughter. Great fat HAW-HAWS and tiny little tee-hees rushed across in a rash of earthy colors and then were gone.

"How many of you are there?" tapped Meg into the keyboard. "What's so funny?"

"As many as you wish!" said the bright green words. "As for who I am, well, I have been a hundred things, in the ages of the world. But you can call me Robin if you like."

"Robin?" asked Meg. "Like Robin Hood?"

"Why, yes!" Robin answered with a sly laugh. "Or Cock Robin, or Robin Redbreast, or Robin Goodfellow. What's your name?"

"Margaret," said Meg, haughtily. "But you can call me Meg if you like."

"Meg?" asked Robin. "As in Nutmeg?"

"Well, no, but—"

"Splendid! Well, Miss Meg, would you care to come with me to Elfland?"

"You bet I would!" said Meg. "What should I do?"

"Just take my hand," said Robin.

"But I can't *see* your hand!" said Meg.

"You're not trying hard enough! Here, let me help. 'Robin Nonesuch, dressed in grass-green silk—'"

"I thought you said your name was 'Goodfellow'," Meg protested.

"It's all the same. Now, where was I? Ah, yes. 'Robin Hobgoblin, attired in shimmering emerald, escorts the fair Lady Megatherium . . .'"

"It's just Meg," said Meg, with a laugh.

"Oh, very well. '. . . leads the fair maiden Meg along a sun-dappled primrose path through the heart of the Green Wood to the court of the Faery queen.' Listen! Can't you hear the soft sound of the wind sighing in the trees and smell the sweet scent of the blossoms blown on the balmy breezes?"

"Kind of," said Meg, hesitantly. And, in fact, she could. For as Robin's words danced across the screen, she found herself caught up in a trance, and she began to hear the sounds and smell the scents Robin described. It was as if she were being led, blindfolded, through a strange and wondrous realm, with Robin as her guide.

"Look!" cried Robin. "There at your feet are pretty little primroses, grinning like tipsy kittens, and far ahead lie the spires of the Faery queen's castle. Can you see it, Meg?"

"Yes!" Meg answered. "Yes, Robin, I can!" For as Meg gazed at the shimmering patterns on the screen, she slowly began to see the path through the Green Wood.

"There, Meg! Just ahead of us is the gateway to the land of Faery! If you listen closely, you'll hear the horns and harps of Elfland and the singing of the Elven host."

"I hear them, Robin! Let's go!"

69

"As you wish, Lady Meg. Come along now, move lively. Mind the troll. Don't trip over that stump. Lift your feet. Don't step in the stream—mustn't get your feet wet, or you'll never get there at all. Wait. We've come to the Faery Ring. Will you enter willingly and without doubt?"

"Of course I will!" Meg answered with all her heart. "Let's go!"

"Very well, then." Robin laughed. "Take my hand."

Meg's fingers tingled. The ghostly music of the Elven court was suddenly louder in her ears, and she could faintly feel the pressure of Robin's hand in her own.

"Here we are!" said Robin. "Oh, look! There's the queen of Faery herself, seated on her gilded throne, with nobles of the Elven court gathered all around her in their finest array. See, the queen is wearing a gown made of violets, and a bright crown of thistles. Isn't she beautiful, Meg?"

"Beautiful," Meg repeated.

"Would you like to meet her?"

"Could I?" asked Meg.

"Certainly. Walk this way. The wood sprites have laid out a carpet of cowslips leading up to her throne. Stand here while the herald announces us. He's quite a sight in his toadskin coat. Very silly, don't you think?"

"Very silly," Meg agreed, feeling somewhat dazed.

"Your Imperial Majesty, may I present the Lady Margaret Mehitable McGillicuddy Malone, late of Middle Earth!" the herald announced in deep, round tones.

"How did he know my name?" Meg whispered. "And what did he mean by 'late'?"

"Never mind that," Robin whispered back. "The queen has summoned us to her throne! Mind the steps. They're steep and narrow. Now curtsy—low," Robin chided. "Where are your manners?"

Confused, Meg did as she was told. As she lifted her head, the Faery queen spoke.

"Come here, child," the queen commanded. Her words were liquid silver, like moonbeams on a field of snow. Meg shivered in spite of herself. "You're a long way from home, aren't you? What brings you here?"

"I'm not sure," said Meg. "I was supposed to go to my big sister's birthday party, but I got sent to my room instead."

"Whatever for?" asked the queen.

"My parents said I'd gotten into too much mischief," Meg said sadly. "They said I'd been so bad, they might not have a party for my birthday tomorrow!"

"Why, that's terrible!" said the queen in a softer voice. The chill in Meg's bones began to be replaced by a numbing warmth. "We never mind mischief here. Well, this won't do. You shall have your party, Miss Megalomania—"

"It's just Meg!" Meg giggled.

"Just as you say," replied the queen. "It will be ever so much fun! It's been so long since we've had one of your kind here. We'll have music, and dancing, and a sumptuous feast of treacle and toast, quail eggs and quince jam, sweetbreads and sparrows' tongues, spiced wines and savories . . ."

"Oh, but I couldn't," Meg protested.

"Oh, but you must!" the queen insisted. "For dessert, we'll have a delicious absinthe sherbet and a

71

lovely cake of lotus blossoms. You'll like that, won't you, dear? Frogmarch! Proclaim the celebration!"

"You don't have to go to all this trouble—" Meg began. But her words were drowned out in a blare of trumpets as the herald began to speak.

"Oyez! Oyez! Be it known to all to whom these presents may come that her Imperial Majesty Tatiana, empress of Elfland and queen of all the Faery realms, has proclaimed this day in celebration of the birthday of the Lady Meg of Middle Earth. May revelry be unrestrained, and may the carousal commence!" The herald's words were greeted by a chorus of cheers and a swirl of merry music.

"This way, my lady!" said Robin to Meg. "Allow me to escort you. This passageway leads under the hill to the queen's palace. Duck your head, now! It's a bit dark. Ah, here we are! Open that golden door, just ahead of you! *No!* Don't touch that one!"

"Don't touch *which* one?" asked Meg, confused.

Robin's voice was suddenly hushed and hoarse. "Be quiet!" he whispered. "Someone might hear you!"

"So what?"

"Hush!" he said. "Listen carefully. I may only tell you this once. There are three doors leading out of this chamber, one green as springtime, one gold as sunlight, and one black as night. The golden door leads to the ballroom and banquet hall of the Elven court. The green door leads back to the Green Wood. You may use either door as long as you are here."

"What about the black door?" asked Meg eagerly, her curiosity aroused.

"It is forbidden to open the black door—or even to

speak of it. More than this, I dare not say. Now come along! The Elven court awaits us!" Robin took her firmly by the hand, pulling her through the glittering golden door.

On the other side, Meg found herself in the midst of a wild celebration. The lords and ladies of the Elven court were frolicking in wild abandon in celebration of her birthday. The sights and sounds went to her head like Christmas punch, and she floated through the banquet hall as if borne on wings of gossamer.

Robin led her at last to a great banquet table laden with dozens of delicacies. She was seated beside the queen, where handsome young men in leafy livery fed her fancy foodstuffs and lovely maidens in flowery gowns plied her with fine wines while Elven musicians serenaded the table.

The food was all delicious, in an ethereal sort of way, but after a few bites Meg's hunger began to ebb.

"No, thank you," she said, pushing away a steaming bluebird pie.

"You must take at least a taste," whispered Robin sternly. "The queen will be most insulted if you refuse!"

"All right," said Meg hesitantly. "But just a taste."

But after that, it was a taste of jellied kumquats, and a taste of pickled porcupine, and a taste of lizard stew; and finally Meg's stomach began to hurt, and she was sure that if she took even one more bite she'd burst like a big birthday balloon.

"No more, please," she insisted. "I haven't got the room!"

"But there's still the cake!" cried Robin. And sure enough, the servers began to bring in an enormous cake ablaze with zillions of candles and surrounded with scoops of sherbet. With a great gasp of breath, Meg blew out the candles while the Elven court sang loud, discordant songs to her health and happiness. Robin sliced her a humongous slab of cake and topped it with a heaping mound of sherbet. Hesitantly, Meg took a tiny bite of each, fearing all the while that she would embarrass herself by tossing her cookies — or rather, her cake — all over the table.

To her great relief, the servers at last began to remove the meal. But a moment later, the drummers and fiddlers and flute players began to play again. Robin appeared at her elbow, taking her by her hands and lifting her effortlessly to her feet.

"Would you care to dance, my lady Meg?" he said.

"I don't know," she said. "I'm not feeling very — "

A moment later they were whirling about the hall, making mad, spinning circles amid the laughing lords and ladies. As the tune ended, Meg tugged on Robin's hand, pulling him toward the table. But then the music began again, and he pulled her back to the dance floor for another round.

It seemed to go on for hours and hours, without any hope of stopping. Meg's feet hurt, her stomach was turning somersaults, and her head felt like it was being pounded with tiny hammers. Finally Meg yanked her hand away and broke out of the circle.

"Wait!" Robin laughed. "Don't go! The night is still young."

"Yes! Stay!" cried the queen. But Meg had had more than enough. Pushing her way through the prancing dancers, she pulled open the golden door and pushed it shut behind her, gasping and panting for breath. Ahead of her was the green door that led back to the Wood. Meg knew she should go that way and try to find her way back to her own world. But she found herself walking toward the black door instead, as if her legs had a mind of their own.

As she drew closer, she could see that there was a great handle of black glass in the middle of the door, carved with creatures that seemed to creep and crawl as she stood there staring.

She was about to turn around and run, but before she could her nose gave a furious twitch and her hand pushed down on the door handle. The door flew open, and a hideous creature with wild eyes and sharp teeth dropped down from above and bit her hard on the nose!

"That will teach you to stick your nose where it doesn't belong!" screeched the creature as it scuttled away. Its words were echoed by a mocking chorus of raucous laughter.

Clutching her throbbing nose, Meg peered around in horror at the room she'd just entered. She was back in the banquet hall, but it was strangely changed. The beauty of Elfland had turned awful and horrid before her eyes. The hall was dank and dingy, draped with cobwebs and soiled with soot. The lords and ladies of the Elven court had turned into trolls and hags. The queen's sweet face had become ugly and sharp, and her eyes had grown dark and cold. Even Meg's dear Robin had been transformed into a grotesque goblin.

Or maybe he'd been one all along.

The laughter of the horrid elves grew louder, and

they began to crowd closer to her, hands outstretched. Meg edged closer to the black door, then turned quickly and pushed her way through it. She started running as fast as she could toward the green door, pushing it open and dashing out into the Green Wood and beyond the hill, without looking back to see if she was being followed.

The wood, too, had turned bleak and dreary, its trees blackened and bare. As she ran through the trees, her flimsy clothing caught on the briars and thorns, and her bare feet splashed through the icy waters of the stream and stubbed themselves on rocks and roots. Finally, she was too tired to run farther, and she collapsed at the foot of a shattered tree, closing her eyes and wrapping her arms around her to keep out the cold. There was a sound like roaring wind in her ears, and the world whirled away in a blur of darkness.

"Meg? Can you hear me?"

Meg's eyes fluttered open. She was back home, in her own bed, propped up against a half dozen pillows and covered by a soft down comforter. She felt weak and tired and hungry, and her feet hurt. So did her nose. Through the half-drawn blinds, Meg could see the first rays of dawn peeking through the trees.

"Meg? Can you hear me?" her mother repeated. At the foot of her bed, her mother and father stood watching her anxiously, with Melody and Maureen standing on either side.

"Of course I can hear you!" Meg said irritably. "Do you think I'm deaf?" She was suddenly afraid they would be mad at her for talking back.

But her mother started crying instead! "It's a miracle!"

"Indeed it is!" her father replied. "Isn't it, girls?"

"A miracle," Mo said softly, her eyes wide.

"A miracle," Mel repeated with a snort.

"What's a miracle?" Meg demanded.

"You're back again!" said Meg's mother. "We were so worried about you, dear."

"Worried about what?" asked Meg, puzzled.

Meg's father put his hand on her shoulder. "You disappeared, Margaret," he said with a sad smile. "You were there one minute and gone the next. But last night you came back to us, and that's all that matters."

"Then you're not mad at me for playing with Maureen's computer?" asked Meg, warily.

"No, Margaret," said Meg's mother. "We're just glad to have you back home, safe and sound."

"Then that means I get to have my birthday after all!"

"No, you don't!" said Mel, smugly.

"What do you mean?"

"You've missed your birthday!" said Mel spitefully. "You won't have another one till next year! I even got the bicycle they were going to give to you!"

"What are you talking about, you little brat?" said Meg.

"You can't call me a little brat anymore," Mel continued, stepping from behind her mother. "I'm as big as you are now!"

Meg stared at her sister, astonished by what she saw. Mel was now as tall as she was, and Mo was nearly a foot taller! "Hey!" said Meg. "What's going on here?"

"That's what you get for sticking your nose into other people's business, Margaret Mehitable!" said Mel. "You were away for a year and a day, and you didn't grow one bit. It's *my* tenth birthday today, and you're still only nine! You're the Baby now!"

BRUCE COVILLE

With His Head Tucked Underneath His Arm

Fifteen kings ruled the continent of Losfar, and each one hated the others. Old, fat, and foolish, they thought nothing of sending the children of their subjects off on war after war after war, so that the best and the bravest were gone to dust before they ever really lived.

The young men left behind fell into two groups: those who escaped the war for reasons of the body — the weak, the crippled, the maimed — and those who avoided the wars for reasons of the mind: those too frightened, too smart, or simply too loving to be caught in the trap the kings laid for them.

This last category was smallest of all, and a dangerous one to be in. Questioning the wars outright was against the law, and standing up to declare they were wrong was a quick route to the dungeons that lay beneath the palace. So it was only through deceit that those who opposed the wars could avoid going off to kill people they had never met and had nothing against.

One such was a cobbler's son named Brion, who had avoided the wars by walking on a crutch and pretending that he was crippled. Yet he chafed under the role he played, for he was not the sort to live a lie.

"Why do I have to pretend?" he would ask his friend Mikel, an older man who was one of the few who knew his secret. "Why must I lie, when I am right, and they are wrong?"

But Mikel had no answer. And since much as Brion hated the lie, he hated even more the idea of killing some stranger for the sake of a war he did not believe in, so he continued to pretend.

One afternoon when Brion was limping through the marketplace on his crutch, he saw an officer of the king's army beating a woman because she had fallen in his path. The sight angered him so much that without thinking he stepped in to help the woman.

"Leave her alone!" he cried, grabbing the officer's arm.

The man pushed Brion away and raised his hand to strike the woman again.

"Help!" she wailed. "He's killing me!"

Brion hesitated for but a moment. Though he knew it would reveal his lie, he sprang to his feet and felled the man with a single blow.

In an instant he was surrounded by soldiers.

Within an hour he found himself chained to a dungeon wall, with no one for company save the occasional passing rat, and no music save the trickle of the water that dripped endlessly down the cold stones.

As the days went by Brion began to wonder if he had been forgotten and would simply be left in his cell to rot. But late one afternoon he heard the clink of keys in the lock. Two uniformed men came into his cell, unlocked his chains, and dragged him to his feet. Gripping his arms in their mailed gloves, they hustled him to the throne room, to face the king.

"Is it true that you refuse to fight for me?" asked the king angrily.

At the moment, Brion's main fight was with the lump of fear lodged in his throat. But he stood as straight as he was able and said, "It is true. I cannot kill a man I have never met for the sake of a war I do not believe in."

The king's jowly face grew scarlet with rage. "Let the court see the treason of this speech. Let it be recorded, so that all will understand why this rebellious youth is being put to death."

Three days later Brion was marched to the public square. His weeping mother stood at the front of the crowd, shaking with sorrow as the guards escorted her son up the steps to the block. Pushed to his knees, Brion laid his head on the block. He heard his father's voice cry out. But the words were lost to him, because the executioner's ax had fallen.

The crowd roared as Brion's severed head tumbled into the waiting basket.

Body and head were buried in a shallow grave far outside the city, in a corner of the boneyard reserved for traitors.

Brion was about as mad as a dead man can be, which may explain why three nights later he climbed out of the ground. Reaching back, he plucked his head from the grave, gave it a shake to rid it of loose dirt, then tucked it under his arm and started for the city.

It was the quietest part of the night when he reached the palace. Most of the guards were nodding at their posts, but even the few who were still alert did not see him enter.

The dead have their ways.

Slowly, Brion climbed the stairs to the king's bedchamber. When he entered the room he stood in silence. But his presence alone was enough to trouble the king, and after a moment the fat old man sat up suddenly, crying, "Who dares to disturb my sleep?"

"I dare," said Brion, "because I know you for what you really are: a murderer and thief, not fit to be a king. You have been stealing your subjects' lives, and I have come to set things right."

Then he crossed the room and stood in a shaft of moonlight that flowed through the window next to the king's bed. When the king saw the body of the young man he had ordered killed just three days earlier standing next to him, saw the severed head with its still raw wound, he began to scream.

"Silence!" ordered Brion, raising his head to hold it before the king's face. "Silence, if you wish to see the morning!"

Trembling beneath his blankets, the king pleaded with Brion to spare his life. "I will do anything you ask," he whimpered. "Anything at all."

The head smiled. Then Brion told the king what he wanted him to do.

The next day the king's advisors were astonished to hear the king announce that the war was over, and that he was calling the armies back from the field.

"Why, your majesty?" they asked. They were deeply disturbed, for they loved their game of war, and were sad to see it end.

But the king would say nothing of his reasons.

Now life in the kingdom began to change slowly for the better. The youths who returned from the war began to take a useful part in the the life of their homeland. With strong young hands to till the fields, the farms grew more productive. Some of those who returned from the wars were artists and poets; some were builders and thinkers. New ideas came forward, new designs, new ways of doing things. As time went on the kingdom grew stronger, happier, and more prosperous than any of those surrounding it.

And in all this time Brion never left the king to himself. Though the guard was doubled, and doubled again, somehow they always slept when Brion walked the halls, as he did every night when he came to visit the king's bedchamber. And there, with his head tucked underneath his arm, he would instruct the king on what to do next.

When morning came, Brion would be gone. But the smell of death would linger in the room. The servants began to whisper that the king was ailing, and would not live much longer. But live he did, and for the next three years he continued to do as Brion told him.

In that time the kingdom grew so prosperous that the other kings on Losfar grew jealous. They began to plot together and soon decided to attack the rebellious kingdom that had left the wars.

"After all," said King Fulgram, "the only reason they have so much is that they have not been spending it to defend themselves, as have we. Therefore, a share of it should be ours."

"A *large* share," said King Nichard with a smile.

When Brion heard that the armies of Losfar were marching on his homeland, he did not know what to do. He certainly did not want a war. But neither did he want to let the outsiders tear down all that had been built. And he knew he could not let them murder his people.

"Send a message of peace to the enemy camp," he told the king, a few nights before the enemy was expected to arrive.

The king sneered, but, as always, did as he was told.

The messenger was murdered, his body sent back as a warning of what was to come.

Panic swept the kingdom.

That night, when Brion stood by the king's bedside, the old man began to gloat over the coming war. "See what you have brought us to," he taunted. "We are no better off, and in fact far worse, than when you started. Before, we fought on *their* soil, and it was *their* homes that were destroyed. In two days time the enemy will be upon us, and this time it is *our* city that will burn."

Brion said nothing, for he did not know what to do.

That night when he was walking back to his grave Brion met another traveler on the road. Brion recognized him as the murdered messenger by the stray bits of moonlight that flowed through the holes in his chest (for the king had described the man's wounds with savage delight).

The messenger turned from his path to walk with Brion. For a time the two men traveled in silence.

Brion felt a great sorrow, for he blamed himself for the messenger's death. Finally he began to speak, and told the man everything that had happened since his own beheading.

"Don't feel bad," replied the messenger. "After all, your heart was in the right place — which is more than I can say for your head," he added, gesturing to the grisly object Brion carried beneath his arm. It was sadly battered now, for dead flesh does not heal, and in three years it had suffered many small wounds and bruises.

Brion's head began to laugh, and before long the two dead men were staggering along the road, leaning on each other as they told bad jokes about death and dying.

After a time they paused, and standing together, they stared into the deep and starry sky.

"I am so tired," said Brion at last. "How I wish that I could be done with this. How I wish that I could rest."

"You cannot," said the messenger. "You must finish what you have started."

Brion sighed, for he knew that his new friend was right. "And what of you?" he asked. "Why do you walk this night?"

"I was too angry to rest," said the messenger. "I wish that those fools could know how sweet life is. But perhaps only the dead can know that."

"More's the pity," said Brion. And with that he left the messenger and returned to his grave.

But the messenger's words stayed with him, and the next night when he rose, he knew what to do. Finding the grave of the messenger, he called him forth, saying, "I have another message for you to deliver."

Then he told him his plan. Smiling, the messenger agreed to help. And so the two men went from grave to grave, calling the dead with these words:

"Awake, arise! Your children are in danger, your parents may perish, your childhood homes will burn. All that you loved in life is at peril. Awake, arise, and walk with us."

Not every soul gave back an answer. Some were too long dead, or too tired, or too far away in the next world. Some had never cared about these things in life. But for many, Brion's call was all that was needed to stir them from their place of rest. The earth began to open, and up from their graves rose the young and the old, the long dead and the newly buried. And each that rose took up the message, and went to gather others, so that two became four, and four became eight, and eight became a multitude, shaking the earth from their dead and rotted limbs, for the sake of all that they had loved in life.

When the army of the dead had gathered at the gate of the graveyard, Brion stood before them. Taking his head from beneath his arm, he held it high and told them all that had happened.

He told them what he wanted of them.

Then he turned and headed for the camp of the enemy.

Behind him marched the army of the dead. Some moaned as they traveled, remembering the sweetness and the sorrow of the living world. Some were no more than skeletons, their bones stripped clean by their years in the earth. Others, more recently dead, left bits and pieces of themselves along the way.

Soon they reached the camp of the enemy, which was all too close to the city. Following Brion's lead, they entered the camp. It was easy enough to pass the sentries. The dead *do* have their ways. Then, by ones and twos, they entered the tents of the living, where they began to sing to them of death's embrace.

"Look on me, look on me," they whispered in the ears of the sleeping men. "As I am, soon you shall be."

When the soldiers roused from their dreams of killing and dying to find themselves looking into the faces of those already dead, fear crept into their hearts.

But the dead meant them no harm. They had come only to speak to them, slowly and softly, of what it is to be dead; how it feels to be buried in the earth; what it is like to have worms burrow through your body.

"This will come to you soon enough," they whispered, extending their cold hands to stroke the faces of the living.

Some of the dead women held out their arms, and when the men cried out and cowered from their touch, they whispered, "If you fear my embrace, then fear the grave as well. Go home, go home, and there do good. Choose life, choose life, and leave this place in peace."

One by one, the terrified men slipped from their tents and fled across the hills to their homes, until the invading army had vanished like a ghost in the night.

Then the army of the dead returned to its graves. They laughed as they went, and were well pleased, and chuckled at their victory. For though they had spoken nothing but the truth, they had not told all that there was to tell. The departing men would learn that in good time; there was no need for them to know all the secrets of the world beyond too soon.

As dawn drew near, Brion stood at the edge of his grave, and stared into it with longing. At last the time had come to discover what came next, the secrets and surprises he had denied himself for three long years.

Tenderly he placed his head in the grave. Crawling in beside it, he laid himself down and died.

DEBRA DOYLE AND

JAMES D. MACDONALD

The Queen's Mirror

When I was very young, my mother the queen had a mirror that hung on the wall in her private chamber. A velvet curtain fell across the glass's gilded frame, but in those days no hand ever drew it aside— save mine, one day when I was curious and, I thought, alone.

My own reflection looked back at me: a girl-child in rich clothing, with the same dark eyes and fair skin that made my mother's beauty famous throughout the kingdom. Behind me, a casement window opened to show the palace gardens and the deep woods of the royal hunting preserve beyond. I saw movement among the reflected shrubbery and turned to find Gregor, the chief of the queen's huntsmen, standing outside in the garden.

I let the curtain drop back across the mirror.

"What are you doing here?" I asked, with all the dignity I could muster. I was always a little afraid of Gregor, who had been in the royal service since the time of my grandmother, the Old Queen — though he must have been a young man in those days, when my mother herself was only a child.

Even now, though silver had frosted the jet-black of his hair and his pointed beard, he bowed with the grace of an ambassador at one of my mother's receptions. "I do the queen's will, Your Highness. And her will is that no one shall enter her chamber while she is away."

He stretched out a hand and I went to him, stepping over the low sill of the window and out onto the lawn. My mother was a kind enough woman, when the cares of state let her remember that she had a daughter at all, but no one in the kingdom would let her commands go by unheeded.

"I will be queen one day," I said when I was safely out of the window and walking with Gregor toward the palace nursery. "Why should I not go where I will? Is it the mirror?"

I thought I saw Gregor's lips smile slightly above his black-and-silver beard. "You're a clever child, Highness."

I smiled at my lucky guess and dared to ask another question. "Why does a curtain hang across my mother's mirror?"

"That was the Old Queen's looking glass," said Gregor. "It was the Old Queen herself who put the curtain there."

Curiosity stirred in me. All my life I had heard tales of the Old Queen, who had ruled palace and kingdom alike with a strong hand, but of all the servants and courtiers in the palace, no one remained from those days save Gregor alone.

"Was she ugly, then?" I asked. "Was that why she hid the mirror?"

"Ugly?" Gregor laughed aloud. "Child, your grandmother had beauty that would make a strong man weep."

We had come by now to the door of the nursery, and I knew that I should go inside, where my nursemaids and my tutors waited. Instead, I sat down on the stone steps and looked upward at Gregor.

"If she was beautiful," I said, "then why would she not look in the glass?"

"She had no need," said Gregor. "She had ladies-in-waiting enough to dress her hair and deck her out with gold and jewels; she could see her beauty reflected a hundred times over in the eyes of the kings and princes who came to her court."

He smiled again, as if he saw them once more in his own memory, those proud and mighty rulers who came bearing tribute and begging favor. I kept myself as quiet and still as the stone I sat on, until his smile faded and he went on . . .

"For twenty years and more," he said, "from the time I first came to serve her until the day when her daughter, your mother, put on long skirts and left the nursery for the first time, I never heard of your grandmother looking in that mirror, nor in any other. But when the kings and princes turned their eyes from the Old Queen to her daughter, your grandmother's temper changed. She grew silent and brooding; her governance of the kingdom became harsher and more unbending. Where formerly her subjects had praised her mercy, now they feared her justice, and in other countries the people who spoke of her called her the Iron Queen.

"Only then," Gregor went on, "did she begin to look in mirrors as if she sought an answer there: the tall mirrors in the palace hallways, the oval mirrors above the palace fireplaces, and always, morning and night, the mirror on the wall of the royal chamber. And at last there came a day when she called me to her.

"She waited alone in her chamber, with her back to the mirror and what it might show her — though to my eyes her beauty was still a fearful thing. 'Gregor,' she said, 'the looking glass tells me I am growing old and ugly.'

"I could only laugh, though more powerful men than I had of late feared to offend the Iron Queen. 'Older, perhaps,' I said; 'we are none of us so young as we once were. But nothing on earth could make you ugly.'

"The answer pleased her, and she smiled. 'Gregor,' she said. 'I believe that you love me well — and I can think of no subject, highborn or low, in whom I can put more faith.'

" 'Only command me,' I said, 'and Your Majesty will see how you are still loved.'

" 'Very well,' she said. 'You are the queen's huntsman; by custom and law you have the power of life and death over whatever the forest holds. I want you to take my daughter into the woods and kill her there.' "

Gregor paused and did not speak again for some time. At last I could no longer keep silent, though I knew that to speak might bring an end to the huntsman's mood and I might never hear this tale again. "But you didn't kill her, did you?" I said. "If you had killed my mother, where would I be now?"

Gregor did not reply or even seem to hear me. It appeared as if he had forgotten me entirely; he gazed outward for a little while more at the dark border of the woods beyond the palace, and then he went on.

"The task was not what I had expected," he said, "and I liked it not at all—but I had not lied to the queen when I said that I loved her well. I chose my finest knife, the one with the polished staghorn grip, and sharpened it to a keen edge for the work I had to do. When the afternoon was almost over I went to the princess, your mother.

"The princess had known me from her babyhood and trusted me; when I asked her to come with me she agreed without question. We went together into the woods near the palace—she laughing at the chance to leave court life behind and play once again at being a child; and I looking about me as we walked for a place to carry out the queen's command.

"But my heart was heavy, and no place I saw could please me: One was too close to the palace and might be observed from the upper windows; another was too bright and cheerful for such a dark deed; and still another was too gloomy and forbidding to be a girl's last memory. Before I quite realized what I had done, the hours had drawn on until dusk, and we had come by unintended paths to the place I knew in my heart we had been seeking all along.

"It was a part of the forest I had passed through now and again but where I had never cared to stay: a clearing in the dark woods, where a low green hill rose up a little way above the surrounding earth. The air was always dim and quiet there, no matter how bright the day or how noisy the forest elsewhere—and now it came to me that here, in the peaceful green shadows, would be a fitting place for the Iron Queen's daughter to sleep her final sleep.

"I took her up onto the top of the mound. She still had no fear—she thought she would look there for the mushrooms that sometimes grow in forest clearings. I stood behind her and drew out the blade that I had taken such pains to sharpen."

This time, Gregor stopped speaking for so long that I thought he would leave the story unfinished, and I saw something in his eyes that might have been unshed tears. I sat silent upon the stone steps of the palace, not daring to open my mouth lest he decide not to continue. When at last he spoke again his voice was lower and more uncertain, as though he were picking his way through a tangle of confusing memories.

"I raised the knife," he said, "and I let it fall. But

even as I struck, the side of the mound opened, and pale women were all around. They pressed close about me, they pulled my hand away, they drew the princess out of my grip and took her to them.

"I could not see their faces, and their voices were like pine trees sighing in the wind.

" 'Give her to us,' they said. 'The queen sent her to the forest. Therefore let her bide in the forest, and we will keep her safe until her own time comes.'

"Slowly, slowly, they pulled the princess out of my arms and took her back with them into that dark place under the earth, and the sighing of their voices died.

"I left the clearing, and with my knife I killed one of the fat rabbits that live in the forest's grassy banks. The blood of the rabbit stained the blade and my hands. When the queen saw me return thus alone, she was pleased and did not look in the mirror for a long time afterward. If the kings and princes who came to her court wondered what had become of her daughter, none of them ever spoke the thought aloud.

"But time passes for all living things, for queens as well as for huntsmen, and there came a time when the Iron Queen grew old in truth. One day she summoned me to her chamber again. This time she stood facing the mirror, and her eyes showed that she had seen everything it had to tell.

"With her own hands she drew the black curtain across the glass and turned to face me. 'Gregor,' she said, 'I have loved you well, and you have been the most faithful of my subjects. Now the time has come when you must do me one last service.'

" 'I am Your Majesty's to command,' I said, though I disliked this speaking of last things.

"The Iron Queen smiled. 'Then, Gregor, I would ask you this: Today at sunset, take me with you into the forest and show me the place where you once dealt with my daughter as I commanded.'

"Her words fell like a heavy weight on my soul—but she was the queen, and I could not refuse. We left the palace at sunset, she and I, dressed as if for a hunting party such as she had enjoyed in the days when we both were young. Again I carried with me the knife with the staghorn handle, and the queen smiled to see it, saying, 'I always knew, Gregor, that you could read my heart—and I trust that your blade has not lost its keenness with the passing years.'

"I would have wept then, if I could, but my throat tightened and I could make no sound. Nor did she speak to me again until we came at last in silence to the grassy mound at the heart of the forest, just as the last of the daylight faded and left the clearing to the gathering dusk.

"She turned to me and unwound the scarf from her neck, leaving bare the white skin that kings and princes had liked to compare to ivory or to new-fallen snow.

" 'Most faithful of all my subjects . . .' she said, and then no more thereafter.

"My hand was steady in its last service . . . and when the deed was done, the side of the mound opened, and the women came to take her away.

"I could see their faces now, even in the darkness—faces white as ivory or drifted snow, with hair black as the night and lips redder than the blood of any forest beast. 'Give her to us,' they said, in those voices that sighed like the wind in the pine branches. 'She has no more need of you, huntsman, and the kingdom has no more need of her. Let her go.'

"I let her go — and what they did with her I never saw. With her leaving, the burden on my soul grew too heavy to bear, and I threw myself face downward on the top of the mound and wept until the morning."

My mother's chief huntsman fell silent then for a long time. From where I sat on the cold steps at his feet, I could see that he was weeping once again at the memory, and he made no move to brush away the streaks of moisture that traced their way down his weather-darkened cheeks. At last he went on.

"When dawn came I saw that the ones who lived in the underground had kept their word from long ago. Your mother was standing above me, her youthful beauty fresh and unchanged from the day I had taken her into the forest at the Iron Queen's command. I knelt before her, and she looked down at me with so much of her mother in her eyes that I trembled to behold her.

" 'Huntsman,' she said, 'rise up and cease your grieving. The Old Queen is dead, and I rule the kingdom now. We must return to the palace and do there what is needful.'

"I was still the queen's huntsman, and sworn to do as Her Majesty bade me. The Young Queen came to her throne before the sun reached its zenith, and she took the kingdom into her hand.

"I feared at first that she would punish me for what I had done at the Old Queen's bidding, but she never spoke of those things or even seemed to remember them. At last I came to understand that the memories had been taken away—not only the memories of that day, but all of her childhood with them; so that I, who had shown her the first spring flowers in the meadows and the secret caches where the squirrels hid their nuts in autumn, meant no more to her than any other faithful servant. But if those who live in the underground had taken away much from her while she was in their care, they had also taught her well. She ruled then as she rules now, with all the strength and wisdom of her mother before her."

That was the story as Gregor the chief huntsman told it, many years past, when I was very young. I thought it strange and sorrowful, but after the manner of childhood I soon forgot it, and likewise I thought no more of the curtained mirror in my mother's chambers.

But time goes by, whether we think of it or not. Gregor is many years dead, and my grandmother the Iron Queen is quite forgotten. My hair has grown long now that once was kept childishly short, and a lady-in-waiting dresses it high on my head each night for dinner at my mother's table, where the ambassadors of foreign kings and princes look at me with curious, speculative eyes.

In the queen's chamber the mirror hangs uncovered. My mother looks into it morning and evening, while at night I dream of voices that sigh like the wind in the pines, and of pale faces watching from the darkness under the trees.

ALAN P. SMALE

The Breath of Princes

She went up.

As the dragon pulled her into the sky and the ground dropped from beneath her feet she saw villagers running out of their houses and emerging from their hiding places. The more keen-witted started putting out the fires while the rest scuttled hither and yon, shouting and getting in the way. She saw Denny, the town Neanderthal, throwing aside his cloak and reaching for a bow. Her father, waving his hands and calling "No! No!" either in sheer distress or for fear that an arrow would accidentally pierce his daughter's breast. Her wicked stepmother, arms folded, staring up at her thoughtfully while the townsfolk boiled around her in panic.

It was all very exhilarating.

Denny shrugged her father aside and brought the bowstring back to his shoulder: *Thwack!*—an arrow glanced off the dragon's throat not a dozen feet from her.

Stephanie screamed lustily. She was of that flaxen-haired, trim, but well-rounded type so popular among agricultural laborers and dragons, and she had good lungs. Mostly, she screamed so that the folks below would know she was still alive and would appreciate a few rescue attempts, but also partly because it was a rather stomach-churning experience to be so far above the ground, with all those arrows flying around to boot. From even this modest height, the circles and squares that made up the village seemed even more tiny and insignificant than they did from ground level. She was glad to be leaving, even in so unorthodox a direction.

The last of Denny's arrows spent themselves harmlessly on the beast's armor, and then the dragon was safely out of range.

As the dragon flew north into the hills Stephanie's vertigo passed, and she watched with interest as the farms far below her gave way to tall pines and log cabins. All too soon even these signs of human habitation became scarce, and she could see a crust of snow on the mountaintops. They were now several days' hike from her village, and the heat from the dragon's body was becoming very useful in keeping her warm against the fresh chill in the air.

Once above the treeline, the dragon headed for a tall, near-vertical cliff face, and soon she could see the irregular hole that marked the entrance to his lair. He slowed his flight as they approached, and he pulled back the foreclaw she was riding on. He was going to lob her into the cave.

"Uh-oh," she said.

For a second the trees spun dizzily below her, then she landed with a bruising *thump*. The dragon peeled off to come around again.

Rather warily, Stephanie got to her feet and turned her back on the dizzying drop. Inside, the cave opened out in all directions as far as she could see. Directly in front of her a straight dragon's length of floor was worn flat and almost smooth; beyond this and out to the sides the floor was more uneven. From an irregular mound to her left came the gleam of gold and the wink of rubies. It looked like the safest and most interesting place to stand, and she headed toward it.

The dragon's giant form loomed into view, traveling as fast as a spear. For a second his great body blotted out the sky, then a rumble like a springtime avalanche split the air as he scoured the cave floor with his belly and slid to a majestic halt in a cloud of dust and a rainstorm of small pebbles. His aroma filled the cave, a potpourri of smells that reminded her of fermenting wine, coniferous trees, damp sheep, and rooms that needed sweeping.

In a confined space the dragon was even more

impressive than before. Stephanie looked at his enormous talons, his scaly hide, his spear-sharp tail. During the landing the beast had held his head so high above the cave floor that he risked scraping it on the ceiling above. Now she saw why; a single scale was missing from the dragon's throat, baring a section of rough hide about twice as wide as she was tall. Now she knew what Denny had been aiming at.

The adrenaline boost of the journey faded away, and she began to feel scared. She avoided the dragon's gaze, fearing that she wouldn't be able to reply if he should speak.

He spoke. "Hello, child."

She had expected to be deafened by a voice that roared like a furnace, and to have to dodge chunks of falling rock as they broke loose in the shock wave. In fact the dragon's baritone was scarcely louder than a small male-voice choir, and almost as melodic.

It was a dangerous moment. She did a wobbly curtsy and said, "Good day." Her voice worked, although it was pitched a little higher than she would have liked.

The dragon sighed, and a coppery breeze wafted by.

"A village is a barbarous place for a young woman-child," he said. "Back-breaking work in the kitchens and fields. Schoolteachers dry as dust, talking of times you'll never know and places you'll never see, filling you with numbers you can't count up to and foreign words you'll never have to use. Boys who pull your hair. Girls who hate you for being prettier if they don't hate you for being uglier. Not much of a life. If you ask me."

Her eyes moved up his body until they reached a

wide, muscular shoulder. Each joint in the giant arm wore its own shield.

"You speak very well," she said.

The dragon grunted. "Missionaries. And previous virgins. But, as I was saying . . .

"What do you have to look forward to? A young man, perhaps. A lover for a year and a master for a lifetime. Children" — and here the dragon leaned nearer as if imparting a great secret— "children, my dear, are very painful. Even after they're born."

She curtsied again. My feelings exactly, she thought. "So I've been told," she said.

"Stop bobbing around, woman-child. So you've been told, indeed. I tell you again, then. But for you, there'll be none of that. I've saved you from such things."

Because of the shape of his head, the dragon could fix her with only one eye at a time. She looked into that eye now: a long yellow slit masking a globe of cool gold. It was the eye of an ice-hearted lizard, and it did not match the voice. As she held its gaze, the eye blinked.

"I'm very grateful," she said.

"Are you?" The dragon moved suddenly, and she stepped back and dropped to her knees, but he was only scratching himself. The eye narrowed. "So. Grateful, indeed. You're glad to be my guest?"

She had, in fact, been loitering conspicuously in large open spaces for the very purpose of being his guest, but it seemed impolitic to say so. Now that she was actually here she was less sure of herself, anyway. "It'll make a change from the normal run of things."

"Hmmm," said the dragon.

She looked around her. Her dark-adjusted eyes could now make out the details of the pile of coins and jewels by her side. Beyond it was a silver suit of armor, empty. Beyond that, a small stream bubbled out of the rock, flowed a few yards along its own little gully, and ducked back into the floor. Unless they were hidden on the other side of the dragon, the cave had no other furnishings.

"You'll sing," said the dragon. "You'll dance. You'll talk to me and tell me jokes. You can clean up a little when I'm out. I get bored with my own company."

She curtsied, forgetting his instruction not to.

"You're a fetching child. Eventually someone may try to get you back. They won't succeed."

"No, probably not."

Little flames dribbled out of the dragon's mouth like molten linguini. "As you say. *Probably* not."

There was an uncomfortable silence. She looked back at the eye. "And eventually?"

"Eventually?" said the dragon.

"In the end?" she prompted.

"Ah. In the end, I'll eat you."

Something moved in her lower abdomen.

"But don't worry," the dragon hurried to assure her. "It'll be a long time before we come to that. And you won't even know when it happens."

And so it came to be. She sang songs of valor and songs of love, children's playground songs, and one or two of the milder drinking songs. She told jokes and recited poetry. She acted out little scenes from plays, doing all the parts herself, as the dragon had a poor memory for lines. She did impersonations of her wicked stepmother and, as her courage grew, of the dragon himself. She danced folk dances and reels, although some of them were tricky without a partner. She rearranged the looser rocks into interesting patterns. While he was out, she washed her clothes and swept the floors. One day, fancying that she saw the tarnish of incipient boredom creeping into the corner of his eye, she began to polish the gold coins in his treasure hoard. He seemed pleased, and she made sure to do them carefully enough that it would take many months to get through the whole pile. She had a knife in her belt—about as useful against the dragon as a handful of gravel but handy for carving small figurines out of the firewood the dragon fetched.

He brought her fresh meat and vegetables, and sometimes milk (still in the cow). He told her how the ancient sagas were recounted among the dragons—the knights never won. He told her how he teased the missionaries. He described his encounters with mythical beings in the badlands, and she scoffed at his fairy stories. He bragged about how his poisoned tail could put a horse to sleep for a decade, and she looked dutifully impressed. She listened to his complaints about yapping dogs and blunt arrows that scratched his armor, and she tried not to scream when he accidentally scalded her with his breath.

Her first would-be rescuer was a long time coming, and she got offended and angry. "I thought I was more popular than *this*," she complained.

"Boys," said the dragon, shrugging. "Always putting things off. No fire in the belly."

She took to standing at the cave's mouth, looking down at the trees far below. Admittedly, it *was* a tough climb. But surely most of the village boys could have done it. And it should have been no problem at all for a prince.

Two years before, the prince had taken a grand tour of the kingdom that would one day be his. By good luck, he passed through Stephanie's village, and by a similar piece of good luck Stephanie fell and twisted her ankle right in front of the royal cart. Wishing to appear kind hearted and a man of the people, the prince got down to assist his subject.

"Are you hurt, maid?" he asked.

She looked up at him and made a snap decision to be bold rather than coquettish. She met his eyes boldly. "I think so, sir. Could you help me up?"

As he bent down, she saw the same look in his eye that she knew from her male classmates' eyes on skiing trips, and she thought, Under all these fine robes he's just like a village boy, really. Which was a distracting thing to think about, for the prince was rather well muscled from swordplay and wearing armor and heavy ceremonial regalia, and he had the fair complexion of a young man who never had to help with the harvest.

As she leaned on him, trying to ignore the *oooo*s of the crowd, she felt his breath on her cheek.

It was a revelation. No hot odors of stew and old milk; no, not he. No brackish wine or muddy coffee smell. A scented breeze of honey and roses issued from his lips, and it was as if the sun had burst through the clouds in midwinter. Princes were indeed a race apart from normal men.

She allowed herself to be helped into his cart, inhaling deeply. There, while she rested, he showed her artists' impressions of his father, the king; the castle they lived in; and the lakes and forests of the far south.

All too soon it was over and he was helping her down from the cart. Their eyes met for a few breathless seconds as she tried to carve her face into his soul, and then he went on his way, leaving her by the roadside.

This little adventure ruined all the village boys in her eyes. She hadn't found them all that appealing anyway, with their breath that smelled of turnips and yesterday's leg of mutton, but she worked on the principle that in one of the adjacent valleys there had to be a youth with broad shoulders who could appreciate moonlight and had learned to pick his teeth clean and chew mint. Now, though, she was a different person. Stephanie had breathed the breath of princes, and nothing would ever be the same again.

When the first of her would-be saviors arrived, it was all over in a second.

She had sung a few songs and was now industriously scrubbing at a large oval coin with an unfamiliar name and crest on it. Suddenly there was a scraping noise and a boy called Nine clambered to his feet in the cave's mouth. He ran forward nobly, brandishing a rough sword and crying out, "For God, Stephanie, and Saint—" and then the dragon's tail whipped around and jabbed him, putting him to sleep and crushing him into the wall at the same time. The torrent of fluid fire that crisped him before he hit the floor seemed almost insulting.

She cried buckets and stopped hoping that village boys would come to her rescue. Nine had been a decent sort, with good muscles but no brain, attributes that had made him ideal to be the first into the dragon's lair. She had not known him well, but it was impossible not to feel sympathy for somebody whose parents had so completely run out of imagination after naming their first eight children.

What had started out being her own personal thrilling adventure was now turning nasty; a boy, however stupidly, had given his life in an attempt to save hers. In a few minutes she aged several years, and the shock made a better person of her, although she didn't think so at the time.

By now her picture should have been all over the kingdom. Where was the prince? Princes were much better at this sort of thing than poor, foolhardy village urchins.

She heard the second suitor before she saw him, and for a while her heart rejoiced. She was cleaning some crud off the dragon's foreclaw when she saw the tail of a rope flick across the cave's mouth out of the corner of her eye.

She began to sing and tap her foot.

Legs. A body. The boy dropped soundlessly to the floor and slid into the shadows, and she almost groaned. It was Colin, the only boy she'd ever kissed (on two consecutive skiing trips). She should have known he would feel honor bound to try his luck, even though he had something of an education; he could at least spell *manners,* although *chivalry* would always evade him.

She found an imaginary blemish behind the dragon's jaw and made him move his head away from Colin so she could excise it. This allowed her to bellow the chorus heartily into his ear.

Colin had a sword, and a good idea where to stick it. He'd seen the missing scale under the dragon's throat. Unfortunately, he lacked the strength to pierce the tough hide.

At the first prick, the dragon jerked his head, bowling Stephanie over, and leered at Colin, who was still rather feverishly hacking away with the sword.

The dragon inhaled luxuriously.

"*No!*" Stephanie shouted.

Colin gave up and fell onto his knees, his face already ashen. The dragon sucked more air.

"No. Absolutely not." Stephanie marched forward and stood between them, hands on hips. "Not this one. He's too good to be charcoal."

The dragon, lungs full and flames licking around his nose, stared at her.

She turned. "Colin," she said. "Thanks. You did well. Now leave."

He ran. The dragon's tail twitched, and she wagged her finger at him. "No! How many times?"

The dragon gulped and steamed a little, then turned his head around the other way. A pent-up column of pure fire poured harmlessly into a rock wall.

As Colin's legs disappeared up the rope with alacrity, the dragon coughed scratchily. The dull glow from the rock cast a scarlet ichor across his scales. His nearer eye was almost completely closed and shone red and furious. For the first time she saw the dragon as a wild, dangerous animal.

The dragon said, "Next time, you both burn. Understand?"

"Yes," she said meekly. "Never again. The next one, the next hundred, all yours." She tiptoed away and hid behind the loot pile.

No more young knights-in-training would show up for a while.

After a day of dark muttering and heavy smoking the dragon said he forgave Stephanie, and things became a little less uncomfortable, but she knew she was living on borrowed time.

She had a feeling that the prince wasn't coming.

The next time the dragon went hunting she looked for Colin's rope, but it was gone. He must have hauled it up after himself when he got back to the ridge. She studied the ground below. Somehow, the trees seemed to be retreating farther into the distance every day.

The dragon stopped laughing at her jokes. He didn't tap any of his feet when she sang. He didn't appreciate her impersonations anymore. She had a feeling she'd made an unfortunate mistake.

Eventually, a third valiant soul dropped in.

The dragon had been taken by the sudden desire for mutton and had gone to look for a plump sheep. She was getting one of the many fire pits ready, so he could cook her portion on his return. Under her breath she was experimenting with some new lyrics, but they weren't going very well. There were not enough words that rhymed with *dragon*.

She didn't notice the new rope flapping in the breeze behind her, nor the solid figure who appeared at the end of it. Her first clue was when she lifted the hem of her skirt to wipe the sweat from her brow and somebody goosed her from behind.

"Wah!" she said, and stumbled, and turned around.

"Hi, Steph," said Denny.

"Oh, not you," she said. "You're the very last person I'd want to be rescued by."

When they were very young, Denny had tickled her till her sides hurt and pulled her hair until she cried. When she was twelve and her body started to change, it was Denny who had turned her crimson with his coarse comments. Denny had grown up taller and more muscular than the other boys, but they were muscles that commanded fear rather than admiration. Even the area between his ears was muscular; he was so far from being able to spell *manners* that she doubted whether he would even be able to spell *sex* without adding superfluous letters.

"That's no way to talk to your *husband,*" he said, and reached out his hand again as the odor of yesterday's meat spilled from his mouth and washed over her. Denny's breath was, without doubt, the ripest in the entire village.

She slapped the hand aside. "Don't make me laugh," she said. "I'd marry the dragon first."

He ignored her. "If you hurry we might get out of here before it comes back. I got a rope. On the other hand, if you want to stay here for a while . . ."

She found herself backing away, with Denny following her around the cave.

"You're crazy," she said. "I can't climb a rope. And he'll be back soon; I don't want to be toasted five hundred feet up a cliff. Besides, I'm not going anywhere with *you*."

"That's fine," he said. "We'll just wait here, then."

"So you *are* mad," she said.

"I've got you," he said, and grinned broadly, revealing a row of brown, cracked teeth. "It likes you. It'll not harm me if I'm holding you."

"Won't work," she said. "I used up all my goodwill stopping him from killing Colin. He's probably right on the verge of having me for dinner anyway. He'll just torch us both."

Did she hear the dry creak of mighty wings?

"All right," said Denny cheerfully. "I'll just have to kill it, then. Actually, I was going to do that anyway."

Against her will, she turned her head to look at the cave's mouth, and Denny grabbed her and clamped his lips to hers, his sword clanging painfully against her hip. Her nostrils filled with a most unprincely stench, and when she slapped him she earned a knock on the side of the head that sent her reeling.

"It's all right," she heard him say. "I don't need your gratitude anyway. Your father—well, he's going to be grateful enough for the both of you."

He seemed very confident for a boy who was about to face a creature that could incinerate a barn from a hundred feet. It was the confidence, she realized, of somebody who had never lost a fight. Unfortunately, she knew he was right about one thing: Her father *would* be stupidly grateful, and she couldn't expect much help from the rest of the village either. They were all too scared of Denny marrying into their own families.

Even Denny could hear the dragon approaching now. As her vision cleared, she saw him walk calmly to the center of the dragon's landing area and pick up an enormous spear that he had left there. Raising the spear at a shallow angle to the ground, Denny braced the haft against a notch in the floor, and she understood. He intended to impale the dragon through the weak point in his throat, using the dragon's own momentum to drive the shaft home. Denny had noticed that the dragon lifted his delicate, uncovered throat away from the ground when he landed at the village, and he'd realized how to make the best use of the one chink in an otherwise impenetrable armor.

She would probably have sat there docilely if Denny's final quiet words hadn't been "Don't worry, Steph. Five or so children will be enough for me." He was staring out of the cave's mouth, watching the approach of the dragon and making small adjustments to the position of the spear. Tucked back as Denny was in the darkness of the cave, the dragon didn't even know he was there . . .

. . . until Stephanie screamed "Look out!" at the top of her voice, picked up the empty breastplate from the treasure mound, and launched herself at Denny.

Her momentum bowled him over and she landed on top of him in an untidy pile. For a second the cave went dark as the dragon's bulk eclipsed the light, then at the last minute she heard the air spilling from one wing as he went into a steep turn.

She tried to hit Denny with the breastplate but he

took it away from her and banged her on the head with it. "What's the matter with you?" he screamed. "Trying to get us both killed?" She couldn't answer, and he dragged her to the cave's mouth, where she dropped on her knees and gasped for breath.

Outside, the dragon was flying in large slow circles, looking irritated.

"Get out of here!" shouted Denny. "Fly away! You can't get at me without harming her too!" The dragon snorted and eyed them balefully as he passed.

"Tell it to go away," he said urgently to Stephanie. "You'd better make it go away, 'cause one way or the other, you're coming with me."

Then he stopped talking, because Stephanie stabbed him with her knife.

In slow motion, he turned to look down at her, astounded at this treachery. She yanked at the blade with both hands, desperately trying to pull it out of his body, but it wouldn't come.

Staring into her eyes, he touched her, almost gently, on the back of her hand. Then he leaned out into space and began the long lazy tumble to the trees far below.

His blood had spilled out over her hand and arm. Her tunic and skirt were red with it. Struck dumb and almost unable to breathe, she sank down until her forehead rested against cool rock, and she wept dark tears while the dragon sailed back and forth on the currents of the air and waited for her to be done.

"Why are you still crying?" asked the dragon later, after she'd finished her story.

Stephanie dragged in a breath. "Because I had no

choice. He was right. Do you understand? My father *would* have given me to him, whatever *I* wanted. He probably didn't really deserve to die. But I couldn't see any other way out. And it wasn't *nice*."

"If you had no choice, then there's nothing to cry about," said the dragon, but she just shot him a glare that would have burned him if he hadn't been fireproof already, and she turned away.

The dragon sat quietly while she washed her face and hands. Finally he said, "Well. I suppose you'd better be going, then."

Fear poked at her but couldn't push its way through the dull ache that filled her mind. "Go on, then," she said miserably. "Make it quick, like you promised."

"That's not what I mean. The village. I should get you back to the village."

She looked blank.

"I can't eat you now," he explained. "You don't qualify as a virgin anymore."

"But he never . . . I . . ."

The dragon breathed in deeply and she cowered, but he was only sighing and hardly any flames came out at all.

"Virginity isn't just about chastity," said the dragon. "It's the state of innocence that's important. I need somebody pure of soul and unsullied by the world. To make up for my own shortcomings. You gave away the things I needed when you took that boy's life."

She thought of all the unpleasantness she'd witnessed during her short life in the village. "If you're going to be that fussy, you'll starve to death," she said. "There's sullying and sullying."

115

"And there's innocence and innocence," said the dragon. "And yours is gone. I can always tell. You're no good to me now, as a meal or as a companion."

"Well, aren't you the virtuous one all of a sudden?" she said scathingly. "You've been killing people all over the kingdom for years and years and years."

"Yes," said the dragon rather patiently. "But I'm not the one who's supposed to be a virgin."

He turned around, ready to launch himself from the cave, and reached out an open foreclaw to her.

She thought of how her life had been in the village — the daily drudgery, the filth, the crude wit, the unclean breath of the boys. And she thought of what she would return to. A husband chosen by her father. A family of her own. She would never leave the village again.

There had been two high points in her life: a few minutes' rest on a prince's cart, and the heart-stopping excitement of flying with a dragon. It was more than most people would ever have, and more than she could ever hope to have again.

"I'm not going," she said.

The dragon's head loomed close. "Indeed?"

She walked to the treasure pile and sat back against it, feeling the hard coins pushing into her. " 'A village is a barbarous place for a young woman-child. Not much of a life. If you ask me.' " She shook her head slowly. "I won't go back to that. Do what you have to do."

The dragon stared at the wall. "You're quite sure about that?"

She nodded. "But don't burn me. I couldn't bear it."

The dragon sighed, spilling golden flame over the rocks near her feet. His head was so close to hers that his single eye seemed to consume her. Did she read sorrow in that eye? She smelled sulfur and heard the scrape as he curled his tail behind her, its razor point carrying a long, long sleep.

She closed her eyes.

And then opened them wide.

"Wait a minute," she said. "I have an idea."

So, one day in late autumn, the dragon set her gently down in the village square and flew away. As the villagers ventured out and marveled at seeing her whole, they heard her proclaim that she, Stephanie, had persuaded the dragon to leave their village in peace from that day forth.

The villagers cheered her — from a safe distance, because it seemed to them that she had grown rather fierce and unfriendly during her captivity. Still, her father was impressed enough by her new bearing not to suggest any possible husbands for a while, and her wicked stepmother treated her with a new respect, and artists' impressions of Stephanie the Dragon Queller spread far and wide through the kingdom. All the boys in the village were in awe of her, and none dared to kiss her on skiing trips anymore, which was just as well.

It was a long, hard winter that choked the roads with snow and kept the villagers indoors around the fire. Since Stephanie had spent the summer coming face to face with death on a daily basis, the petty intrigues of the village held no interest for her. She watched the small, unimpressive flames fluttering in the grate, and she waited for springtime.

At long last the snows melted and the kingdom re-opened for business.

Soon after, while she was doing some sewing, the needle quite by chance escaped her grasp and fortuitously buried itself in her soft flesh. As a single bud of ruby red blossomed on her thumb, Stephanie laid her head on a handily placed pillow and fell into a deep and glorious sleep.

Her stepmother, who was no fool, sniffed the needle and smiled.

Once again the artists' impressions circulated around the kingdom, and this time her fame was too great for even the prince to ignore. In a few weeks his cart swept into the village square and he strode regally into Stephanie's hut and kissed her on the cheek, and of course nothing happened at all, because the magic of dragonsleep is more powerful than mere superstition.

Somewhat embarrassed, the prince had her slumbering form lifted onto his cart and took her back to the castle in the far south and summoned his best healers, who came up with a cure and overcharged the prince royally for it. And Stephanie awoke with the scent of honey and roses filling her nostrils, to find herself in the royal castle with a rather smug prince at her side and a bevy of jealous ladies-in-waiting looking on.

She won over the prince with a single sparkling smile. The ladies-in-waiting took more work, but she was equal to the task. After a while, charming dragons becomes a way of life.

JANE YOLEN

Harlyn's Fairy

Harlyn had not expected to see a fairy that day in the garden. Buttercups, yes. And the occasional early rose. And varieties of plants with odd names like snow-in-summer and bachelor's button. Aunt Marilyn loved to plant and grow flowers, almost as much as she liked to watch birds. But if she had ever seen a fairy in her garden, she had neglected to tell Harlyn about it.

Yet there it was, flittering

119

about on two fast-beating wings as veined and as transparent as stained glass. It sounded like a slightly dotty insect and was pulling the petals off the only red rose in bloom.

Harlyn drew in a sharp, surprised breath. When she exhaled, the wind nearly blew the fairy halfway across the arbor.

"Whooosh!" the fairy cried out. When it had gotten its tiny wings untangled at last, it flew back toward her, shaking its fist and scolding in a voice that sounded as if it were being run backward at the wrong speed. Harlyn didn't understand a word.

After a half-minute harangue, the fairy flew down to the ground and picked up the dropped petals, stuffing them into a silvery sack. Then it zipped off in the direction of the trees, canting to one side because of the sack's weight.

But how much can rose petals possibly weigh? Harlyn mused.

When the fairy disappeared into the copse of trees, Harlyn turned.

"Oh, Aunt Marilyn," she said aloud, "boy, do you have some explaining to do."

"A *fairy?*" said Aunt Marilyn, shaking her head. "Don't be silly, child. It must have been a ruby-throated hummingbird. They move that way." Her hand described a sort of twittery up-and-down zigzag motion not unlike the fairy's flight pattern.

"A fairy," Harlyn said. "It spoke to me. Well, yelled, actually."

"And what did this *fairy* say?" Clearly Aunt Marilyn did not believe her.

"How should I know?" Harlyn answered. "I don't speak Fairy. But it wasn't happy, that's for sure."

"It was pretty hot out there, dear..." Aunt Marilyn began in her *understanding* voice, the one she'd used since Harlyn's mother's latest breakdown brought Harlyn once again to her house.

Harlyn nodded, though they both knew the day was really on the cool side.

"How about a peanut-butter sandwich?" That was all Aunt Marilyn was going to say about the fairy, of this Harlyn was sure.

Harlyn ate the sandwich and drank a glass of milk while Aunt Marilyn hovered over her, carefully watching for signs of something like the delusions Harlyn's mother had entertained on and off ever since she had been a teenager. Harlyn was well aware of this scrutiny; she even welcomed it, usually.

"It *was* hot out, Aunt Marilyn, hotter than at home. And there were *lots* of birds," Harlyn said at last.

"Nothing else?" This was Aunt Marilyn's way of offering a truce without actually saying the dreaded f-word, *fairy.*

"Nothing else," Harlyn answered.

"I have to go shopping, and you can come with me if you want to..." Aunt Marilyn clearly wanted to shop alone, and Harlyn was really too old to need a babysitter, having already done a bit of sitting for other kids herself.

"I'd rather stay home," she said. "I brought a book." She had *The Hobbit,* which she was about to read for the fourth time.

Aunt Marilyn sighed and picked up her pocketbook and binoculars. "I won't be long."

She will, though, Harlyn thought, especially if an interesting bird suddenly crosses her path.

As soon as the car left the driveway, Harlyn bolted out the back door and into the garden. This time the fairy was harvesting handfuls of mint from the herb patch. The little silvery pack was almost full.

Turning her face carefully to one side so as not to breathe on the fairy, Harlyn watched it out of the corner of her eye. Clearly it knew she was there, for she was much too big to be ignored. It ignored her nonetheless.

"Can I help?" she whispered.

The answer was as indistinguishable as before, high pitched and foreign and fast, but Harlyn took it as a *yes.* She knelt down and began to pull bits of mint leaves off, tearing them into tiny pieces that she handed to the fairy. The fairy took them, not at all gratefully, and tore them into even smaller bits, then stuffed them into the pack until it was overflowing. Then, without so much as a wave, it flew off.

"Well—thanks to you, too!" Harlyn called after it.

She said nothing about seeing the fairy again when Aunt Marilyn came home. And what with one thing and another—making Tollhouse cookies and peanut-butter pie and helping Aunt Marilyn put stamps in her albums—the day flew past. At bedtime Harlyn borrowed a bunch of bird books, knowing that—though they had wings — fairies were certainly not birds. Probably not even a related genus or species. But the books were worth checking out anyway.

Besides, it pleased Aunt Marilyn, who didn't like Harlyn reading books like *The Hobbit*. She thought fantasy stories were trashy, even dangerous, and said so often. "Empty make-believe" was one of her favorite phrases.

Harlyn checked through the section on hummingbirds with special care. They were certainly the right size, and their wings beat as quickly as fairies' might. So it was just possible that . . .

"Nuts!" Harlyn said aloud. "It *was* a fairy. It spoke to me and it was carrying a bag." Besides, her mother's delusions were about people trying to kill her and UFO aliens kidnapping her. Crazy stuff. Harlyn put the book down. She knew what she'd seen.

Harlyn dreamed all night of hummingbirds who called her name, and of eagles the size of roses quarreling with the hummers. When she awoke, the sky was gray and rain was slanting down so hard that the rose arbor looked as if it were behind a very dirty curtain.

"House cleaning," Aunt Marilyn said in a cheery voice. "That's all you can do on a day like this."

Harlyn thought wistfully of her book. She was at the riddles part, which she loved. But it wouldn't do to make a fuss. That would mean a well-intentioned lecture from Aunt Marilyn with unsubtle references to living in fantasy worlds. So Harlyn helped clean.

It was while she was working on the windows over the kitchen sink, the ones usually kept open for the robin who had adopted Aunt Marilyn, that she found a pink rubber band and three red berries, dried and shriveled, set side by side. Harlyn didn't want to climb off the counter just to throw them away, so she shoved them into her pocket, meaning to dump them when she was finished with the windows.

"And what," she said to herself as she scrubbed at one particular spot on the windowpane, "have I got in my pocketses, my precious?" She hissed with gusto, like Gollum, or like an overworked kettle. But by the time she'd finished the windows, she'd forgotten to throw out the berries.

In the afternoon the rain ended and a glorious rainbow settled over the arbor. The lawn was so damp, Harlyn went out barefooted, but she couldn't find the fairy anywhere. Not even a trace of it.

Though what could be considered a trace of a fairy? she wondered. Torn rose petals? There were plenty of those. A second rose, a yellow one on a different bush, had opened, and the wind accompanying the rain had beaten off some of its petals, scattering them like a miser's treasure onto the lawn.

It was just when she had decided there was no fairy to be found and her imagination had indeed gotten the best of her that Harlyn heard a strange, tiny, thin wail, a meager thread of sound. It was not *like* anything, or at least not like anything she had heard before. She followed it, rather as if winding it up around her finger, until she came to an old and shaggy birch tree at the edge of the garden, in the untidy "natural" part she liked best, which ran down to a little stream.

The sound was louder now, but not any more robust, and Harlyn cast about for whatever was making that sound. For a moment the sound seemed high, then it was low, then somewhat oddly in between.

And then she saw a line of ants — rather large ants, about the size of her knuckle, the stinging kind, dark and purposeful — marching around the tree's trunk. They had been disguised at first by the birch's dark patches, but soon she could distinguish them against the white. They were heading toward the thicket on the right, where there were mean and wicked-looking thorns. When Harlyn squinched her eyes, she could see that the ants in front were carrying something tiny and light colored. She bent over and stared and, at last, realized that what they were carrying was a teeny tiny baby — no bigger than her pinkie nail — wrapped in a yellow rose petal. The baby was waving its little arms and crying. It was that crying that Harlyn had heard.

Suddenly the grown-up fairy simply materialized above the marching ants, dithering at them and swooping and swerving overhead, shaking its tiny fist and screaming. It tried several times to snatch the baby, but the ants fought it off fiercely each time, hardly pausing in their march toward the thicket.

For a moment Harlyn watched, fascinated. They were all so small — ants and fairy and baby — that she could hardly feel anything but amusement at first. But then the fairy saw her and broke off its chittering attack on the ants to fly her way, waving its tiny arms and haranguing her again in its high-speed language. Without thinking, Harlyn put her hand out and the fairy alighted on her thumb.

125

When Harlyn brought her hand to her eyes, she could see that the fairy was unmistakably female — probably the baby's mother. And she was crying and yelling at the same time.

"All right. All right," Harlyn said. At her voice the fairy was silent. "I'll see what I can do." She waved her hand gently, which sent the fairy sailing back into the air.

Harlyn snapped off a dead branch of the birch and, using it as a kind of a whisk broom, tried to brush the closest ants away. But as if they had some dark magic binding them together, they scattered for a moment and then re-formed their line, marching on and on with the fairy child toward the thicket of prickers and humming an evil-sounding ant chant.

Harlyn tried a second and a third time with her stick broom, then angrily tried stomping on some of the ants. But each time she did, they scattered and returned.

The fairy flew up by her ear and chittered loudly at her.

"Well, I don't know what *else* to do!" Harlyn shouted back, loudly enough to make the fairy shove her tiny hands over her tiny ears. "I mean, it's like they have magic or something. And I don't. You know — *magic!* Ugga-bugga-abracadabra-zam-booie!" She waggled her fingers.

The fairy went "Oh-ah!" in a high-pitched voice and suddenly fluttered around her three times at a speed that made Harlyn's eyes cross. And at each turning, the fairy sprinkled Harlyn with some kind of powder that must have been mainly ragweed because it

made Harlyn sneeze and sneeze and sneeze until her
nose dripped and her eyes filled up.

"Enough already!" Harlyn cried, wiping a hand
across her eyes. When she could see again, everything
around her seemed awfully green.

And awfully big.

But that was wrong. What she meant was, she
seemed suddenly and awfully small. And she hadn't felt
anything, except—well—the sneezing. Of course she
wasn't as small as the fairy, who was still raging at her
and flinging the powder this way and that, but she was
small enough so that the grass was suddenly like a high
fence all about her and the marching ants in front of her
were as large as motorcycles—and looked as dangerous.

"Oh, great, you stupid fairy!" Harlyn shouted. "I
might have done some good at my regular size. But
what am I going to be able to do when I'm this small?"
She grabbed up a nearby stick—it would have been a
twig if she were at her regular height—for protection.
Then she swung it wildly at the ants. They scattered
again, all but the front three. Of course they *would* be
the biggest and meanest looking. And they were the
ones taking turns carrying the baby.

"Oh, great!" Harlyn said out loud, for the three
were heading purposefully and unrelentingly toward
the thicket and she could hear the rest of the ants starting to re-form behind her. Pretty soon she would be an
ant sandwich. It was not a pleasant thought.

And then she remembered . . . and flung the stick
aside.

"What *have* I got in my pocketses, my precious?"
The rubber band had gotten proportionately smaller

with her, but it still had its stretch. She pulled on it to test its bounce, then reached back into her pocket for the three hard dried berries. Planting her feet firmly, she pulled out one of the berries, dropped it into the sling, and let fly toward the three ants carrying the fairy's child, screaming out all the movie war cries she could think of: "Geronimo! Cowabunga! Heigh-ho, Silver, you ants, and away . . ."

She wasn't quite as accurate with the slingshot as she was with spitballs, the berries being both larger and heavier than the rolled-paper wads she was used to. But the berry dropped like a bomb on top of the middle ant's head, startling it so it dropped its hold on the baby and ran off to sulk in the grass. The other two ants, though, grabbed up the little bundle and, as if of one mind, marched on urgently toward the thorns.

Harlyn bit her lip. "Okay, you suckers," she whispered, putting the second berry in the sling. She let fly. It caught the left-hand ant on the leg.

The ant dropped its hold on the blanket and began to walk in circles.

Harlyn dived forward, shouting, "Say uncle, you ant!" and laughing at the same time, mostly because she was scared stiff.

The lead ant was now inches from the thicket, and from this close the thorny entrance looked sharp as doom. Harlyn put the last berry in the sling and was about to let it rip when something bit down on her ankle from behind. It stung like stink.

"Ow!" she cried, reaching down. The last berry dropped out of the sling and rolled away. Harlyn kicked back with her injured leg, connecting with the ant's head. Then, hobbling forward, she grabbed up her stick again and jammed it between the lead ant's jaws and the yellow rose-petal blanket. Surprised, the ant opened its mouth and the baby dropped out.

There was a swoosh of wings and the mother fairy slipped down startlingly fast on a quiver of air, grabbed the child before it hit the ground, and winged back up without a by-your-leave. And there was Harlyn, left all alone to face a line of large, angry ants.

"What will Aunt Marilyn say?" Harlyn wondered briefly. Even more briefly she wondered, "Will Mother think the space aliens got me?" Then she hefted the stick like it was Robin Hood's staff and prepared for her final fight.

Just as the line of ants closed in, chanting and snuffling and breathing out some kind of dark, thick smell, a fine mist began to fall and Harlyn started sneezing and sneezing, again and again and again.

Blinded by the tears in her eyes, she felt her way backward, somehow eluding the line of ants, until she reached the trunk of a tree. Quickly she crawled around the back. Then she managed to creep into a corner of a crevice between the roots.

She must have slept, tired from the fight or the allergy attack, because she could only faintly hear the fairy shouting at her, "Harlyn . . . Harlyn . . ." When she opened her eyes, she realized the voice was really Aunt Marilyn, calling from the door. Harlyn's leg ached and she was unaccountably dirty and . . .

"There you are," Aunt Marilyn said. "I've been frantic. I couldn't find you anywhere, and then there was this enormous infestation of horrible gigantic ants that seemed absolutely immune to my spray, and . . ." She paused and ran a hand through her thick grey hair. "And now, sweetie, a call from the hospital saying your mom won't be released anytime soon."

"Not coming home," Harlyn whispered. She was surprised she did not feel worse.

"And look at your leg! That's some bite. Did those ants get you? We need to put something on it at once. Their bites can trigger allergic reactions, you know."

Aunt Marilyn took Harlyn inside and soaked the bite in peroxide, which hurt, but not exactly, and then put antibiotic cream on it, which felt good, but not exactly.

"I could just kill those ants, sweetie," Aunt Marilyn said.

"I know you could," Harlyn said. She gave Marilyn a hug, then, as there was still some time before dinner, went back out into the garden.

By the tree was a twig, and twined around its top in a complicated knot was the rubber band. At the base of the twig were red rose petals. The whole thing looked very much like some sort of memorial. A line of very large ants were carefully avoiding the site. Of the fairies — mother and child — there was no other sign.

"Empty make-believe?" Harlyn whispered aloud. "Space aliens?" Then she shook her head. She knew better. But she wouldn't tell her mother or Aunt Marilyn. Especially Aunt Marilyn. After all, Harlyn expected she would be living here for a good long time, and it would be better to protect her aunt from anything as real as a fairy.

VIVIAN VANDE VELDE

Lost Soul

She was sitting on the rock, smiling to herself, her feet dangling in the stream, and he thought she was the loveliest sight he had ever seen. She leaned backward, bracing her feet on the rock, and arched her back so that a handspan or two of her long hair dipped into the water, where the current gently tugged at it. She closed her eyes against the brightness of the sun, but still she smiled. It was wonderful to see her, he thought, to see someone so obviously in love with life.

She straightened, laughing, and shook her head so that crystal beads of moisture flew in the afternoon light. Her hair was the color of the wheat ripening in the field he had inherited when his father had died.

The wheat, a little voice reminded him. It was time for harvesting the wheat. There was work to be done, which he had put off to visit his ailing grandmother, half a morning's walk away from home. He had stayed as long as he could but left because a harvest cannot wait. Though he was eighteen years old and though he had spent his entire life helping his father, or planting and harvesting on his own, at the moment he found it difficult to remember what it was he needed to do.

This forest was said to be haunted by spirits eager to devour an unwary man's soul. But he was a Christian and he knew a man's soul was his own, so he stepped out from the trees and into the clearing.

Still smiling, she gazed directly into his eyes.

He had thought she might be startled. "Excuse me," he might have said then. "I didn't mean no harm," he could have said, and come forward to show that he was, in fact, harmless. Something—something—to get started. But she only sat there, her eyes as cool and green as the stream, the smile still on those pretty lips.

"Ahm . . ." he said, and could go no further without shuffling his feet and twisting the cap he clutched in his sweaty hands—just like the time ten or eleven summers back when he'd been caught pitching pebbles at the swans in the baron's moat.

She tipped her head and looked at him quizzically. "Yes?" she asked, still smiling.

A lady. He could tell by the way she said just the one word. A lady, despite the unbound hair and the bare feet and the plain green dress trailing in the stream. And here he was coming up to her in the woods, bold as anything, and her people no doubt just a shout away, ready to come tearing out of wherever they were waiting for her and beat him for his presumption.

"Uh," he said.

"Oh," she said. "I see. *Ahm. Uh.* That must be how you charm the girls — by telling them such sweet, pretty things."

He felt his face go red, despite the fact that she had still never stopped smiling. "No," he mumbled.

"No?" she repeated. "*No,* you don't charm girls, or *no,* you don't tell them sweet, pretty things?"

He had no idea how to answer in a way that wouldn't make him out to be a fool. "Ahm . . ."

"Oh, back to *ahm.*" She leaned back, supporting her weight on her arms, stretching slowly and deliberately.

He forced his gaze back to her face and saw that she was well aware of where he had been looking. And was pleased by it, he realized with a jolt of surprise, just as she patted the rock and said, "Come and sit by me, boy, and tell me some more sweet, pretty things."

Boy. Even though he was a man by any standard, with his own holding, which he had farmed successfully for almost two years now. Even though they looked to be much of an age. For the briefest instant he was angry, but she was still smiling at him, and he was finding it hard to breathe.

Because of the way she was sitting, he would have to step into the stream to get around her to the other side of the rock. Should he take off his boots? It only made sense, but then she would see that his feet were dirty and callused. She whose feet were white and smooth and beautifully shaped. He tore his gaze from her feet and stepped — boots and all — into the water, which was colder than he had anticipated. There was an undercurrent too, so he teetered out of balance and sat more quickly than he had intended.

"You're sitting on my hair, boy," she said.

"I'm sorry," he breathed, and stood long enough to brush away a long, golden strand. It was soft and smooth and fine and it smelled wonderful—*she* smelled wonderful: like the first day of spring after a hard winter.

She leaned forward to wring the edge of her dress, and her arm brushed against his. He didn't dare move. She looked back at him over her shoulder, then fanned the skirt of the dress, exposing long, shapely legs. Her skin was pale.

Like ivory, he thought. Not that he had ever seen ivory, but "skin like ivory" was what the ballad singers always said. So much more beautiful than the tanned legs of the girls in the village or those who worked their fathers' holdings.

She left the hem up near her knees. "You're shivering, boy," she pointed out. "The water's not that cold."

It wasn't. But he said nothing.

"What's your name?" she asked.

"Quinton." He cleared his throat and repeated it.

She laughed. " 'Fifth-born,' " she said, which he already knew from the baron's chaplain. "Are you?"

It took a moment for the question to sink in. He nodded.

"How delightful." She laughed, and he ached from the beauty of the sound, though he had no idea why she laughed. He had never met anyone who talked like this, who acted like this.

"What's your name?" he asked.

Her green eyes sparkled as she looked him over. She waited just long enough for him to regret his brashness before she answered, "You may call me Salina."

"Salina," he murmured, trying out the sound of it.

"Do you like it?" she asked. "I just made it up." She put her hands around the back of her neck and lifted the mass of her hair so that it brushed against his arm. "It was very wicked of you to sit on my hair, Quinton," she said.

"It was an accident." Don't be angry, he begged mentally. "I didn't mean it."

"Of course you did, you wicked boy. You wanted to touch my hair."

"I didn't," he protested. "I swear."

"You didn't?" She looked at him soberly. "Don't you like my hair?"

"I . . ." Was she angry or not? "Yes," he whispered. Oh, definitely yes.

"Then you may touch it again." She turned her back to him, so that he was bedazzled by the sunlit

135

goldenness of the hair. A waterfall of silken threads. She wasn't angry after all.

His hand shook, touching her shoulder.

"Now, Quinton." She looked back at him. "I said my hair."

He didn't know whether to say *Yes, Salina,* or *Yes, my lady.* So he only said, "Yes," and combed his fingers through her hair and was grateful that she couldn't see his rough, sun-browned hands.

She made soft, throaty sounds of approval and, after a long while, leaned against him, her hand resting lightly on his leg. He couldn't believe his good fortune, that this was happening to him. Her breathing was slow and regular, while his came faster and he had to concentrate to remember to keep his mouth closed. She was a lady, he reminded himself; he could lose everything by trying to go too fast. He worked his fingers upward, then let his hands linger on the back of her head, massaging. And when she seemed to like that, he strayed forward, to rub her temples. She settled more firmly against him, rubbing her shoulders against his chest, so he moved his hands down once more to her shoulders.

She whirled around and slapped him. "That's enough now," she said.

He sat back, surprised and dismayed. Had he been too rough? Or had she suddenly discerned what was on his mind? She had to have known, he thought. She had to have known what effect she was having on him.

She was shaking her hair out and rearranging her dress. He couldn't tell what she was thinking.

"Please," he whispered.

She didn't seem to hear him.

He looked away and saw that the sun was low in the sky. Almost dusk—where had the time gone?—and he was only halfway home. When he had first sat down he had brought his feet up onto the side of the rock, but somehow, without his having noticed, they had ended up back in the water. They felt numb with the chill.

"Well?" Salina said.

He looked up.

"Will you be my gallant champion and carry me back to dry land?" She held her arms open, and very, very gently he picked her up. The current tugged even more strongly than he remembered, but she held tightly to his neck, which almost sent him into a panic of ecstasy.

Once back on the grassy shore, she asked, "Are you going to set me down, or will you hold me all night long?"

"Do I have a choice?" he asked.

"Silly boy. You *can* talk sweetly. Put me down."

He did, ache though he did to do so.

"Will you be back tomorrow?" she asked.

His heart thudded so hard he was sure it was about to burst. "Yes," he said. "Oh yes. Will you?"

"Perhaps," she said, "Quinton. You'll just have to come back and see." She turned quickly and walked into the woods.

"Wait." He took several steps, but already she was gone.

She didn't appear to have taken the path toward

Woodrow, where his grandmother lived, nor the path toward his own Dunderry.

"Salina," he called into the darkening woods. She could be anywhere and he wouldn't see her in this light. "Lady Salina."

But all he saw was the dark bulk of the trees, and all he heard was the whisper of leaves.

It was dark by the time he reached his cottage on the forest side of Dunderry, but somebody had gotten a fire going inside: he could see the light around the edges of the door. Who? he wondered. Both his parents were dead, and the two sisters who had survived childhood had husbands and children of their own and wouldn't be here.

Salina, he thought, beyond all reason.

He flung the door open, and a dark-haired peasant jumped up from the pot she was tending over the fire. "Quinton!" she cried. "Are you all right?" She threw her arms around his neck, and for the longest time he couldn't think who this young woman might be.

"Ada," he said finally, pulling the name from a far corner of his memory. She smelled of stale earth and was suffocating him. He pulled away.

"Quinton?" Her voice grated despite the concern in its tone. "Did your grandmother . . . You were gone so long. She didn't . . . What happened?"

Did she know how ignorant she sounded? Did she know how stupid she looked with that worried expression? But that wasn't fair; she was only trying to be helpful. It wasn't her fault she was so dark and ugly and common.

"My grandmother?" he repeated.

"Quinton? Your poor sick grandmother, she didn't . . . die, did she?"

"No." Quinton looked into the pot of stew Ada had made for him. Beans and onions. Salina wouldn't have made him a supper of beans and onions.

"Quinton," she demanded.

"What?" He looked up at her. "My grandmother is fine."

"Then where were you? We were expecting you back by midafternoon. Where are the baron's draft horses?"

The horses. Now Quinton remembered. He was supposed to have brought the horses for the harvest tomorrow. He, Ada's father, and several others with holdings in the baron's northern lands were going to work together. "I forgot."

She gave him that dull, uncomprehending look again.

"I'll get them tomorrow."

Would she ever close her mouth?

"I forgot!" he screamed at her. "I'll get them tomorrow. I can't very well go now." Did he have to pick her up and throw her out the door to get her to leave? He remembered the feel of Salina in his arms and moaned.

"Quinton?" Ada sounded scared.

He got into the bed in the corner without even taking off his boots. He pulled the cover up to his chin although the night was warm enough to go without, and he turned his back to her. "I'm all right," he said, to get her to leave. "I'll get the damn horses tomorrow."

He heard her hesitate, then take the pot off the fire,

then leave. He clutched the blanket and thought of
Salina.

At first daylight, he set out without breakfast. He
saw Ada's father cutting through the wheat field but
didn't pause. "I'm getting the horses," he shouted,
waving, not stopping.

"Quinton!" he heard Hakon call, but he kept on
walking. The baron's castle was to the east, but so was
the stream where he had seen Salina. He'd go there
first, then on to the castle afterward.

He didn't know how he had made it through the
night without her. He hadn't slept at all. He had to see
her again. Had to smell her. To touch her. Please be
there, he thought. Please be there.

She wasn't.

It was still early. Perhaps he should have gotten the
horses first. Maybe she would come only in the afternoon. He watched the sunlight sparkle on the stream
and didn't dare leave for fear he'd miss her.

He lay down in the grass, torn between enjoying
and being afraid of the sweet ache of thinking of Salina. She'll come back, he thought, and I'll see that she's
not all that I remember. Pretty, but there are a lot of
pretty girls.

He'd get over it. He'd get her out of his mind. Nobody, nobody could look that beautiful. Skin could not
be that soft, that pale and radiant. Eyes could not be so
green and deep. Hair, lips, throat could not be that perfect, that inviting. To touch her just once, just once . . .

He woke with a start.

His face was pressed against the grass, but he could see that the moon was out, pale and low, sharing the late-afternoon sky with the sun. He lifted his head, turned to face the stream.

Salina was there, though he had not heard her come. She was sitting on the rock, in the same green dress, watching him with that day-brightening smile.

"Sleepy Quinton," she called. She stretched, standing on tiptoe, so that her tight-fitting dress seemed to cling to every curve of her body. Then she stepped onto the grass, standing close enough that he could have touched her. "I could easily grow to love you," she whispered. "In fact, I may love you already."

Before he could catch his breath, she disappeared into the trees.

"Salina!" He jumped to his feet. But she was already gone.

He had waited so long, to see her for such a short time. It wasn't fair. It wasn't fair.

He waded out into the stream, to the rock upon which she'd been sitting. It was still warm. He thought he could still smell the fresh scent of her there. He sank to his knees so that the cold water came up to his chest, and he put his cheek against her warmth on the rock.

By the time he got back to the cottage, night had once again fallen. Ada was waiting there for him, again, but this time so was her father.

"Quinton," Hakon said, putting a big hand on his shoulder and shaking him with a little less friendliness than his tone indicated, "Quinton, lad. What ails you?"

"Nothing," Quinton said. His clothes had not dried in the night air and he was shivering.

"You're fevered, lad."

Quinton pushed the older man's hand away.

"Where've you been?"

Quinton shrugged and turned his face from Ada and her father.

Hakon wouldn't be stopped. "I went to the castle," he said.

The horses. Quinton had forgotten yet again.

"I saw nary a sign of you along the way, and the second stable master said they'd not seen you either."

"No," Quinton said. He started to get undressed, hoping that would get them to leave. He kicked his boots off, then pulled his shirt up over his head.

Ada turned her back.

"I brung the horses," Hakon said.

Quinton took his pants off and crawled into bed, and still Hakon stood there staring at him.

"We done Rankin's holding in what was left of the day. We're doing Durward's tomorrow morning. And Osborn's and Halsey's, if we have the time. If you want yours done the day after, you'll be at Durward's with the rest of us."

Quinton didn't answer, and eventually the two of them left.

She wasn't there the next day, though Quinton got to the stream early and didn't leave at all. He spent the night out in the open, sleeping on the grass where she had stepped on her way from the rock to the forest. The next day dawned misty and rainy, and by late afternoon he was too cold and hungry to wait any longer.

At home he found a pot simmering over the fire. Ada. Wouldn't that girl leave him alone? As a matter of principle, he wanted not to eat what she had prepared; but principles don't ward off a chill. He ate the soup and the bread and crawled into bed.

"Salina." He said the name out loud, as though that would have more effect than just thinking it. "I hate you," he whispered into the night. "Come back. Come back." Tears ran down his face and he was too tired to wipe them away.

The next morning, Hakon was there before Quinton had a chance to leave. "Quinton," he said. "We're willing to give you another chance."

Chance? Quinton thought, fastening his boot. Chance?

"You having some kind of woman trouble?"

Quinton snorted, shifted to his other boot.

"Ada — Ada, she been outside your door last night. She said to her mother she heard you calling some woman's name."

"It's none of your business, old man."

Hakon grabbed his arm. "See here," he said, all pretense of concern, of friendliness gone. "You done made promises to my girl. Certain things are expected of you."

"Leave me alone."

Hakon held on to him.

I could easily grow to love you, Salina had said. In fact, I may love you already. She was no doubt waiting for him even now. And this old fool was keeping him from her.

"Let go of me!" he cried.

"You're not going nowhere," Hakon said. "You're going to stay here and work your father's holding and do right by my girl."

Quinton snatched up the heavy pot in which Ada had cooked the soup. "I don't want your ugly little daughter," he said, shoving the pot at Hakon. "Take this and get out of here."

"You damn well better want her," Hakon said. "I'll go to the baron. I'll tell him what you promised and he'll see to it you marry her proper or lose your rights to this land."

Quinton didn't care about the land. He didn't care about anything except getting out of there, of getting to Salina. But Hakon wouldn't let go. Quinton swung the pot and hit him across the side of the head.

The old man dropped.

Quinton straightened his shirt, which had gotten pulled down over his shoulder. Salina, he thought. Salina was waiting.

Shortly before he reached the edge of the forest, he heard footsteps running up behind him. "Quinton," a female voice called. He turned and faced her: a dark girl, unlike his Salina of the sunlight. She had dark eyes, dark hair, even her skin was darkened by years of toiling under the sun. Soon, in another few years, it would be wrinkled and cracked and sagging—youth did not last long in the northern holdings. He couldn't put a name to the girl who clutched at him and begged him to return.

"Who is she?" this ugly walnut of a girl demanded. "Nobody lives in the forest, Quinton. Not real people.

You've found some wood sprite or a naiad, one of the old folk."

He kept on walking, though she had pulled his sleeve loose at the shoulder.

"Quinton, she'll steal your soul away."

That was ridiculous. A soul was a soul. How could it be stolen away, like a loaf of bread or a pair of boots? He didn't bother to tell this girl that. He told her, "Look to your father."

"Quinton?" She stood there with that vacant expression on her homely face, looking from him to his cottage, back to him.

Once he saw that she wasn't following him into the woods, he didn't look back.

He found Salina where he'd first seen her: on the rock by the stream. But this time she wasn't alone.

There was a young boy with her, sitting on her rock in what should have been Quinton's place. A peasant, he saw. An ugly, dirty little peasant. He was an overgrown child of perhaps thirteen or fourteen, and he was finger-combing Salina's beautiful golden hair.

"Salina!" Quinton cried.

She turned, languorously, to look over her shoulder at him and smile. "Quinton," she said, her voice as empty as her eyes and her smile. "My pretty-speeched young sleeper. Have you dreamed of me lately?"

Quinton strode into the water, fighting the pull of the current. The peasant boy didn't even have the decency to appear frightened of him. His eyes were dull and unresponsive and he continued to comb his fingers through Salina's hair as though unaware of anything else. Quinton's gaze went from Salina's lovely face past her shoulder, down the length of her arm, to her hand resting on the boy's thigh. Apparently she wasn't concerned that he was ugly or little more than a child.

Quinton grabbed him by the collar and hauled him off the rock, staggering against the pull of the current. He flung the young peasant into the water, in the general direction of the shore. At least the boy had wit enough to scramble to his feet.

"Tomorrow," Salina called to him. "Come back tomorrow."

The boy ran off into the forest.

Quinton looked from his retreating back to Salina and saw his life collapse in front of him. "You said you loved me," he said.

"I lied," she told him.

"But I love you."

"I know."

"Please—"

"Don't beg," she snapped. "Begging is for cripples and dogs."

"Salina . . ." He broke off at the look on her face.

"Boy?" she said, laughing.

"I gave up everything for you."

"And I have nothing to give you in return." She held her arms open. "Did I ask you for everything?"

"Don't laugh at me," he said, and she laughed at him again. "Don't you laugh!" he screamed. And still she laughed.

He grabbed her by the hair and dragged her into the water. She didn't even struggle, she was laughing so hard. He pushed her backward and held her down so that her face was under the water, and even that didn't get the smile off her face. Her hair streamed out, looking green and feathery. And the smile never left her face, even long after she had to have been dead.

He staggered to the shore, repulsed by what he had done, repulsed because of the sense of exhilaration he felt, repulsed because he didn't know if that had come from being pressed against her or from killing her.

I'll go back to Dunderry, he thought. He remembered Ada's sweet face and thought with horror of the way he had treated her. He'd tell her . . . He remembered her father and sank to his knees. Had he struck the old man hard enough to kill him? There was no way of telling. Not without going back to see.

"Hey!" a voice called.

He jerked up his head to see two men on horseback. The baron's guards, judging by their chain mail.

"You Quinton Redmonson?" one of them asked.

"No." He shook his head and backed away. Hakon must be dead. Ada must have gone to the castle and told them what had happened. "No," he repeated. He felt the incline of the ground where it dipped down to the stream.

The man pointed a finger at him. "You. Get back here."

Could they see Salina's body? he wondered. He couldn't. Had the current carried her away already? He could argue that killing Hakon had been an accident. But would they believe two accidents in one day? The cold water lapped at his ankles, his knees.

"I said — "

But he missed the last of what the baron's man said, because his foot slipped in the muck at the bottom of the stream and he fell. For an instant he came up sputtering, then the water closed over his head again.

It isn't this deep, he thought. It isn't this deep. He was facing upward. He could see the sunlight hitting the surface of the stream, but he couldn't get to it.

The water roared in his ears, pressed down against his face. Salina, he thought. Salina was holding him down. But that was foolishness. There was nothing there. All he had to do was sit up. It was only the water pressing down on him. Water no deeper than Salina's hair was long. Water that pressed down on him until he didn't want to sit up after all.

He stopped struggling. He let the water in. Up above, the sunlight danced a golden green dance. The last thing he saw was her, the last thing he thought of was her.

She was sitting on the rock, smiling to herself, her feet dangling in the stream, and he thought she was the loveliest sight he had ever seen. She leaned backward, bracing her feet on the rock, and arched her back so that a handspan or two of her long hair dipped into the water, where the current gently tugged at it. She closed her eyes against the brightness of the sun, but still she smiled. It was wonderful to see her, he thought, to see someone so obviously in love with life.

DAN BENNETT

The Way of Prophets

Ransom sat on a stump and
wrestled his left boot off his
aching foot. He turned the boot
over and shook out a cloud of
dust.

He looked around. In the
past six hours, the wide gravel
road that people called the Way
of Prophets had narrowed and
turned rough; now it was little
more than a rat-scurry cutting
through the thick, high grass
between the trees of the
Yardling Forest.

149

He had taken a wrong turn.

"Definitely," he said to himself, adjusting the straps of his heavy backpack. "A wrong turn. Or two."

He started to put his left boot on, then thought better of it. Instead, he took his right boot off and began rubbing his sore feet.

All this walking had worn an evil-looking blister on his right heel. He glared at it, an ugly blemish on his otherwise perfect, uncallused foot.

"This," Ransom said, "was not part of the deal."

As he understood it, the deal was this: He'd been born the first child of the twenty-seventh king of the Stuard Isles. That meant he had certain princely duties—and certain privileges.

Until six days ago, those duties had consisted mostly of sitting in Stuard Castle on a bejeweled, velvet-padded chair beside his father's throne, drinking red wine from a golden goblet, and smiling roguishly at the young ladies of the royal court until they blushed and looked away.

But that was six days ago.

His seventeenth birthday had brought plenty of pleasant surprises—a strong white stallion to train for the next Harvest Games, a new cloak of red velvet so dark it looked almost black, a kiss from each of the young noblewomen he'd been stringing along.

But not all of the surprises were pleasant.

His father took him aside and explained the deal:

"For seventeen years, you have had a fine and easy life, Ransom," his father said.

"And why shouldn't I?" Ransom had thought. "I'm the prince, after all." But he didn't say anything. It was clear his father wanted to lecture him, and it was Ransom's experience that the best thing to do when adults were talking was to keep quiet, smile and nod, and pretend to be interested until it was over.

His father continued: When a member of Stuard royalty reached his or her seventeenth birthday, he or she was expected to journey alone on the Way of Prophets, an ancient road that ran from Stuard Castle, on the east coast of the Isle of Stuard Kings, all the way across the main island. It was a two-week walk, even under the best conditions, and legend held that the young ruler-to-be always found his or her destiny as king or queen before reaching the west coast.

Ransom's grandmother had made her journey in late fall, just as an early freeze killed the last fruit on the trees and forced the rabbits underground. By the time she reached the western shore, she was so weak with hunger she could barely stand. When she took the throne and became queen, her first official act was to have extra granaries and food cellars built to help her less fortunate subjects survive the hardest winters. And that was only the beginning. She devoted her life to feeding her people.

Near the end of his own journey, Ransom's father was set upon by bandits who beat him within an inch of his life, took his money and his clothes, and left him wearing rags. His first decree as king created the Stuard Militia, a well-trained, well-armed force that supported the sheriff of each county in the kingdom. Already, he was known as King Eduard the Just — harsh but fair, he took a personal interest in maintaining law and order in his kingdom.

"For most," Ransom's father said, "it is a symbolic journey." The original Way of Prophets had been lost for ages, he explained. Most young nobles walked the new road, but legend had it that, once in a great while, a ruler-in-training would be allowed to find a path to the true Way of Prophets. This always marked a critical point in Stuard history.

Ransom had convinced himself that he would be the one to find the true Way. He had believed since he was a child that he was destined for greatness.

But now he was nearly halfway into his journey, and so far it appeared his destiny would be to lead the people of the Stuard Isles into a wilderness where they would all become hopelessly lost.

He'd been lost before, as a child in the hedge-maze on the grounds of Stuard Castle. But he'd had a bell with him then, a brass bell as big as his two fists put together. The chief gardener had given him the bell before he entered the maze, and when he got lost, all he had to do was ring it until the gardener found him and led him back out.

But Ransom didn't have a bell now — and there was no one around to hear it, anyway.

Bong-bong. Bong-bong.

"Yes," Ransom thought. "That's what it sounded like."

Bong-bong. He could almost hear it.

Bong.

He *could* hear it. A bell. And it wasn't only as big as his two fists. It was too loud for that. As big as his father's throne, maybe.

It was the sort of bell that hung in a tower. The kind you used to call people from all around. And since Ransom had no idea where he was going anyway, he pulled his boots back on, turned toward the ringing sound, and started walking.

In a few minutes he topped a hill and saw it: Nestled in the valley just ahead was a white abbey with a tall bell tower. Ransom thought it was beautiful, and not just because it was the first sign of civilization he had seen in six days.

Despite his sore feet, Ransom broke into a run. By the time he reached the neatly kept dooryard in front of the abbey, his breath was rasping in his throat and he had just one thing on his mind.

A cool drink of water.

Since the start of his journey, Ransom hadn't come across a single source of drinking water — not a spring, not a stream, not so much as a shallow puddle. He carried water with him, of course — but it was stored in a wineskin made from a goat's hide. As a result, all his water was lukewarm and tasted as if it had recently passed through a goat.

But the abbey would have a well or an underground cistern full of water cooled by the earth.

A cool drink of water.

Ransom's mouth might have watered at the thought, had it not been so dry.

Ransom lifted the huge brass knocker, and he was about to let it drop when the door swung open. The little man who stood in the doorway wore the simple brown robes of a monk. He had thin white hair and a long beard that made him look as if he could have been a thousand years old.

"Young Prince Ransom," the old man said. "Please come in."

Ransom hesitated. "Have we met, sir?"

"Oh no," the man said. "But I know who you are, and I knew you were coming."

"But I only found this place by accident," Ransom said. "Even *I* didn't know I was coming here."

"Very little that happens in this world truly happens by accident," the old man said with a smile. "Please follow me."

He turned away, and Ransom followed him into the abbey.

Just inside the door, three monks were busy cleaning the stained-glass windows and polishing a wooden floor that already gleamed like the surface of a mirror.

The old man led Ransom through a twisting series of candlelit corridors lined with stunning tapestries depicting various scenes: a young prince on a dusty trail, a goblet that shone with a mystic light. They passed through dozens of doors. In every room it was the same: monks hard at work shining silver candlesticks, polishing brass bells, dusting wooden railings, making the abbey look more beautiful than Stuard Tower on a feast day.

"The brotherhood has been preparing for your coming for three hundred years," the old man said. "As the abbot, I have watched for omens of your arrival all my adult life. When I awoke this morning, I knew today was the day."

"You're a prophet, then," Ransom said.

"Of course. You *were* traveling along the Way of Prophets, Prince Ransom."

"But I got lost —"

"You lost the new road, only to find the old," the abbot said. "You have found the *original* Way of Prophets. The true Way, which few men are privileged to travel. And here you are."

Ransom's heart swelled. He had been right, after all. Now he was sure he would be the most important ruler in Stuard history.

They had come to a pair of huge oak doors reinforced with wide iron bands. The old abbot gave the doors a little push, and they swung wide without the slightest creak.

Beyond the doors was a magnificent chapel. Stained-glass panels set in its vaulted ceiling let sunlight fall in bright pillars onto the altar at the chapel's center. An impeccably clean red carpet ran from the doorway down the aisle, between rows of benches, and up three low steps to the altar.

The benches were packed with robed monks — hundreds of them. They all rose silently when they saw Ransom and the abbot.

"Please come and take your rightful place at the altar," the abbot said, and he led Ransom down the aisle.

The monks averted their eyes and fell to their knees as Ransom walked slowly past them.

"All this is for *me?*" Ransom said.

"These men have devoted their lives to preparing for your arrival. This is their greatest moment."

"Excellent," Ransom said. And he thought, "Now, this is more like it."

The old man smiled slyly. "I knew you were going to say that," he said.

"What?"

"A little prophet humor," the abbot said. "Sorry."

Finally, they came to the altar. On it sat a large silver goblet.

Ransom remembered his thirst immediately.

"Is that for me, too?" he asked.

"Naturally," the abbot said. "Take it and drink your fill."

Ransom grabbed the goblet and brought it to his lips to drink.

Water. Not ice cold, but cool enough. A cool drink of water.

Ransom tipped the goblet up and drank until it was empty.

Behind him, Ransom heard a rustling. He set the goblet down and turned to face the benches. Most of the monks were already walking out unceremoniously; others appeared to be dismantling the benches and carrying them off. Two more were bent over the red carpet, rolling it up.

"What's happening?" Ransom asked the abbot.

"It's over," the old man said. A hint of sadness colored his voice. "After three centuries, the prophecy has been fulfilled. The Brotherhood of the Cool Drink of Water is no longer needed in this world."

Ransom had to step away from the altar as four burly monks lifted it and carried it away. The abbot walked out of the chapel, and Ransom wandered after him, bewildered.

In the corridors, monks were taking the tapestries down from the walls and packing the silver candlesticks in boxes.

"But, sir!" Ransom called after the abbot.

The old man turned around, looking slightly annoyed. "You're still here?"

"Yes," Ransom said. "I thought—it's just that I still have a long journey ahead of me. I thought perhaps I could rest here tonight, and—"

"Certainly not, my Prince," the abbot said. "The rest of the prophecy remains unfulfilled. The Way of Prophets awaits, and you must waste no time."

Without another word, the old man stepped through a side passage and shut the door in Ransom's face.

A few minutes later, Ransom found himself standing outside the abbey, looking west along the true Way of Prophets. He was too confused to think anymore, so he started walking.

Ransom walked the rest of the day, as the sun slid slowly out of the sky and toward the horizon. When his shadow had grown long behind him, his stomach began to growl.

There was no traffic on this legendary road, so he sat down in the middle of the Way of Prophets to take his evening meal.

Ransom opened his pack. He took out a bit of salt-cured fish and a bundle of dried sparrowgrass wrapped in linen.

His father, the king, had taken care to see that Ransom had plenty of the sort of rations a traveler should carry. The problem was that traveling rations were barely worth the effort it took to carry them, much less chew them.

He bit into the fish, winced at the stinging, salty flavor of it, and spit out a small bone.

"What I wouldn't give for a half-decent meal," Ransom muttered through a mouthful of the dry, fishy-tasting stuff.

And he heard another bell.

Ransom was on his feet in an instant. He paused just long enough to grab his pack and sling it over one shoulder, then he ran down the road toward the sound of the bell.

Around the next bend stood a gray stone tower that looked older even than Stuard Castle, which he believed had been standing since the beginning of time. A huge bell swung in a belfry at the top.

Even before Ransom could knock, a sweet-looking old woman opened the tower's heavy iron door.

"Young Ransom!" the lady cried joyfully. She wore the white hooded cloak of a holy woman, and she bent her knee and lowered her head in a little curtsy.

"You expected me," Ransom said unnecessarily.

"Why, yes," the woman said.

Ransom was beginning to understand. "I was hungry," he said. "I was thinking of food. Then I heard the bell, and . . ."

"You need sustenance for your journey, my Prince," the woman said. "The ladies of the sisterhood have been waiting for hundreds of years to play our part in the prophecy. And here you are!"

"I knew you were going to say that."

"Pardon me, young sir?"

"A little prophet humor," Ransom said, feeling pleased with himself. "Listen . . . Honored Matron, the prophecy awaits. Perhaps we should go ahead and fulfill the sisterhood's part of it?"

"Indeed, my Prince," the woman said. "The prophecy speaks of your wisdom."

She stepped aside and bowed again, waving Ransom into the tower.

The heady aromas of a busy kitchen took his breath away as soon as he walked through the doorway. He recognized scents he hadn't encountered in far too long: roasting meat, spices, baking bread—

His stomach growled loudly. The old woman pretended not to notice.

She led him to a chamber at the center of the tower's ground floor. Ransom wasn't surprised—or particularly impressed—by the great domed ceiling, the polished walnut table that stretched the length of the room, or the attentive rows of white-cloaked women, young and old, who gazed at him reverently.

Before each woman sat a silver dish piled high with sliced roast turkey, little potatoes smothered in gravy, fresh greens, and buttered rolls the size of cannonballs.

At the far end of the table was an empty chair. Ransom walked quickly toward it without having to be told.

"Roast turkey," Ransom said. "Very nice. I prefer

goose, but I don't suppose you get it this far west."

"Oh, but we've prepared a *special* meal for you," the old woman said proudly. "One that fits the prophecy perfectly."

Ransom's mouth watered uncontrollably as he sat down. What kind of meal could be worthy of a centuries-old prophecy?

A pretty young woman set a covered silver platter in front of him. As she lifted the shiny domed cover away, his heart skipped a beat.

And then his heart sank.

On a small pewter plate in the center of the platter sat a cold sandwich—a slab of flabby ham and a leaf of lettuce between two slices of coarse brown bread. Beside it sat a brass cup filled with milk.

"Honored Matron," Ransom said, trying hard to hide the disappointment in his voice, "I'm wondering . . ."

"Yes, young sir?" the woman replied respectfully.

"The sisterhood—are you by any chance . . ." He thought hard for a moment. "Are you the Sisters of the Half-Decent Meal?"

"Why, yes!" The old woman beamed. Several others dipped their heads to hide a blush of pride.

"That's what I thought," Ransom muttered.

It *was* what he had said, after all. Right before the bell rang, he had said to himself, "What I wouldn't give for a half-decent meal."

It made a kind of sense. And because he had no one to blame but himself, Ransom sat in silence and politely ate his sandwich while the sisters feasted on roast turkey.

Not until the meal was over — and the sisters were serenely cleaning and packing the silver, preparing to abandon the tower now that their work was through — did Ransom speak up again.

"Honored Matron," he said, "what can you tell me of the prophecy?"

"Why, little more than you already seem to know, young sir." The old woman was packing straw around a crystal punch bowl in a sturdy wooden crate. "I knew the sisterhood's part in your destiny, of course, but — "

"But as for what that destiny might be . . . ?"

"I know nothing. I am truly sorry." Her look of regret lasted a second, maybe two, and then she was waving a hand at something on the floor behind Ransom. "Could you bring me that saucer there, my Prince?"

Minutes later, Ransom found himself facing west once again, walking alone along the Way of Prophets. The sun had sunk well below the horizon, and only the moon lit his way.

Trudging along in the dark, Ransom soon became aware of how exhausted he was. Each step was an effort. After an hour or so of walking — most of it uphill — he decided it was time to turn in for the night.

Searching by moonlight, he soon found a clear spot on the ground beneath an old tree. He also found that he could hardly bear the thought of sleeping on the soil another night, especially now that he was up in the Middle Hills of Stuard Isle, where the ground was colder and harder than ever.

"Anything but this again," he said to himself as he spread a thin blanket over the dirt. "I'd settle for a straw mat—"

In the distance, a bell rang. Ransom winced.

That night, Ransom slept fitfully and uncomfortably in the Temple of the Straw Mat. All around him, a hundred acolytes of the temple rested peacefully on thick mattresses of goose down, covered with woolen blankets.

The next morning, Ransom could've kicked himself—and he would have, if every muscle in his body weren't stiff as a board from spending a night on the floor of the temple, separated from the cold stone tiles by no more than an inch of brittle straw. In his condition, it was all he could do to keep walking westward.

"You have to be careful what you wish for."

His father had told him that a hundred times, and it seemed that old saying was especially true when you traveled the Way of Prophets. The people who lived along this road had seen Ransom's every thought years before he was born, and they apparently had a talent for picking his most ill-considered wishes and making them reality.

Ransom figured he could get just about anything he wanted, as long as he was careful about his wishes.

And as long as there was another temple or tower full of prophets around the next bend in the road.

That gave him an unpleasant start. Ransom knew magical things often came in threes. What if the Temple of the Straw Mat had been his last chance? What if he had journeyed all this way only to waste his every chance at something special?

No. He had to be here for a reason. No one had walked the true Way of Prophets in so long that it had become lost and forgotten. He hadn't stumbled upon it simply by accident, and all those prophets and acolytes hadn't been waiting all those years just to fulfill a few silly wishes.

At the very least, he could wish for something he truly wanted. But what did he really want? He thought hard and kept walking.

A fine horse? He had just been given a stunning stallion for his birthday, as strong and fast and wild a horse as he ever could have hoped for.

New clothes? He'd gotten plenty of those, too — so many, in fact, that he doubted he'd have time to wear them all before his *next* birthday came around.

A pretty girl? No — plenty of beautiful young women visited Stuard Castle every day, and he knew any one of them would be his wife if he just winked in her general direction. That tended to take some of the enjoyment out of it. But for now, he was having too much fun just flirting with all of them.

But there had to be something he wanted, something that wasn't automatically his simply because he was who he was, the next king of the Stuard Isles.

Something that wasn't guaranteed.

That sounded familiar, Ransom thought. His father had once spoken to him of such things.

"There is only one thing you are not guaranteed as king," he had said in a rare moment alone with his son. "When I am gone, when you take the throne, you *will* be powerful. That is guaranteed. Your knights and armies will make sure of it. And you *will* be loved and respected. That, too, is guaranteed. No matter what you say and do, there will always be those ready to smother you with love and respect, if you let them, simply because you wear the crown. Because of who you are, Ransom—because of who you will become when I am gone—you need never be hungry or alone.

"But there is no guarantee that you will *matter*. That is the one thing that even a king must earn. Throughout Stuard history, there have been kings and queens who did little more than keep the throne warm for their successors. They gave no thought to improving the world around them, so they were forgotten soon after they died. For all the power they held, they were less important in the long run than the lowliest shepherd's apprentice."

Ransom heard his father's voice echo in his head, and in that moment he knew what he wanted.

A moment later, a bell began to ring in the distance. Ransom ran toward it as if he had just begun his journey.

An armored sentry met him at the gates of an ancient fortress set alone in a grassy clearing. From one of the watchtowers, Ransom could hear a huge bell still humming from its last loud peal.

"Greetings," the man said in a deep, dignified voice. "I am Sir Aaron. The knights are honored to welcome any traveler of the Way of Prophets. Our order has waited hundreds of years—"

"Yes, I know all about that," Ransom said, anxious to get to the point. "I'm Prince Ransom."

"Oh, I see," the knight replied. "Then you must know that, one day, young Princess Grania will venture along the Way of Prophets, limping painfully — "

"Limping? Who is Grania?" Ransom asked impatiently.

"I'm sorry, my Prince," the knight said. "I assumed you already knew about Princess Grania. She of the Blistered Feet."

"She of the — what does that have to do with my wish?"

"Your wish, sir? I am afraid I do not understand."

"My wish was to be important."

"Indeed," the knight said, a look of reverence coming over his face. "And what could be more important than serving the prophecy?"

"Serving the prophecy?"

"Yes, my Prince. The knights have been without a leader for quite some time. And you, with your royal blood and kingly education, are the perfect leader for our order."

Ransom stroked his long, graying beard and looked out at the setting sun from an upstairs window in the old fortress. It had been years — decades, even — since he had sent one of the knights to Stuard Castle to tell his father he wouldn't be back to assume the throne. His destiny had always been here; he knew that soon the waiting would be over.

Soon Princess Grania would come limping down the Way of Prophets on her way to her destiny, wearing boots with the high, narrow heels of the fashion that had lately swept the courts of the Stuard Isles. Her feet would be badly blistered from several days' walking in these boots, and she would be cursing herself for her foolishness.

And wishing for just one thing.

On that day, the destiny of the Knights of the Sensible Shoes would finally be fulfilled.

Ransom sighed contentedly. It was good to matter.

SHERWOOD SMITH

Faith

"My dog can talk."

Fay said it like it didn't matter as she fell into step beside us, her round shoulders hunched into her old purple coat.

"What?" Both Melissa and I yelled it.

Fay shoved her lank blond hair behind her neck and nodded, still no sign of a smile on her face. "Yup. Probably won't last long, but it's fun."

"How did that happen?" I asked.

"Saw a triple shooting star, so I did this ritual I read about."

Melissa was silent.

I hurried into speech. "What's he said?"

Fay shrugged, the worn seams of her coat straining, as she sidled a glance at Missy. "Dog stuff."

Melissa still said nothing.

We'd just crossed to the school parking lot when the principal's voice ripped out at us. "Reed!" Melissa flinched, and I jumped, but Fay just hunched tighter, looking kind of like a rock on legs.

"Faith Reed, come here!" Mr. Conley was standing on the steps just outside the gym building, watching the students come to school.

Mr. Conley glared at us until we were right next to him. "Reed, has your mother seen that memo?"

"Yes, Mr. Conley," Fay said, her voice the thin, flat one she always used with adults.

"Well, where is she?" he roared.

"She's in the hospital, Mr. Conley," Fay said.

"What?"

"Foot problem, Mr. Conley. Waitresses get it. She'll be out soon."

The principal stabbed a finger toward her face. "Your brother," he said, loudly enough for everyone in the parking lot to hear, "is going to flunk out unless we get some cooperation. One graduate to four flunk-outs is not a good record, even for you Reeds. You just pass that on."

"Yes, Mr. Conley."

The principal glared at Melissa, then me; even

the furrows in his face looked mean. All around us, kids were silent, looking sideways, no one coming near.

"Go to class," he ordered.

We hurried away.

"Is your mom going to be okay?" I whispered.

Fay gave her head a shake. "Nothing wrong with her. Matt's problem, not mine."

We ran up the steps, into the relative safety of the corridors. Around us, kids yelled and screamed, lockers slammed, and bodies rushed by.

Melissa said, "I think it's *humiliating* that he should single us out like that, for something that isn't even our fault."

I knew why the principal had done it — to make Melissa and me feel embarrassed, so we'd stop hanging out with Fay. Teachers had tried it, too, but they were usually sneakily nice and reasonable about it. Mr. Conley didn't have to be sneaky. No one stood up to him, ever. Our parents were still afraid of him, just as they'd been when they were in school.

Our lockers were right in a row. "Library after school?" Fay asked, looking at both of us. "You don't have ballet, Missy, and I know *you* don't have band practice." This last was to me.

"But I might," I said. "Mrs. Lopez threatened us with extra practice if we can't get that jazz thing right. Of course, maybe a miracle will happen and we will," I said.

"I can't," Melissa said quickly. "Madame has invited me to observe the senior technique class. I can learn a lot that way."

"Oh." Fay hunched a little further into her coat. "Okay."

We walked in silence toward homeroom, Melissa and I to Mr. Kent, A–L, and Fay on down the hall to Mrs. Nashimura, R–Z.

As soon as Fay was gone, I said to Melissa, "You can watch the seniors do ballet any day, can't you?"

Melissa rounded on me. "She lied to us." Her blue eyes were fierce, her pretty mouth tight. The only reason the three of us hadn't been made fun of long ago was that Melissa was the prettiest girl in the school, and probably the most talented. Looking around now, she dropped her voice to a whisper. "I don't care if she lies to Conley, or even to teachers. But not to *us*."

"You mean about the dog?" I'd almost forgotten it, after that scene with Mr. Conley. When Missy gave a short nod, I said, "She's just doing some kind of story-game. Like being an alien and the Middle Earth Radio thing."

Two years before, Fay had had this idea that an alien had traded bodies with her. She'd done it to everyone, and we'd gone along with it. Missy seemed to enjoy it as much as I did, same as when Fay had announced the summer before that she had found a radio station that tuned in to Middle Earth and for a while brought us news, every day, about the doings of the Fourth Age Gondorians and Hobbits and Riders of Rohan.

"She knows it's not real," I said. "It's just acting — like she did just now with Conley." I knew as soon as I said it that this had been a mistake.

Before I could start on the difference between games

and realities, Melissa opened the door. "Then maybe it's time to stop," she said over her shoulder, and she went into the classroom, her head queen high, her skirt swirling around her long ballet-trained legs.

A group of boys watched her, and one of them said something that I couldn't hear, but she ignored them, dropping her books onto her desk.

I realized I was still blocking the doorway, so I went in. Of course no one noticed me—something I was glad of, for I had to think.

It was the first time Melissa had ever said anything outright that meant the friendship might break up. Lately she'd been getting busier and busier with her ballet, while last year we met at the library practically every day. Before that, we'd met at the park and played out our versions of stories we read or saw. But now it was changing; the two most important people in my life were pulling away, and I didn't know how to fix it. I felt sick inside, much worse than Conley had tried to make me feel—and then I'd only felt bad for Fay.

At lunch we sat together, as always. But instead of story talk, Melissa went on brightly about tests, and teachers, and even the weather. I did my best to keep that stupid conversation going. Instead of talking, Fay was quiet. In fact it was hard to look at her, sitting there so short and square in the ugly old coat all of her sisters had worn—after they, too, got it as a hand-me-down.

I ate as fast as I could and tried to get things back to normal as I held out my lunch bag to Melissa. "I'm full," I said. It was my turn to have leftovers. "Anyone want that extra ham sandwich?"

But then Melissa put her bag down on the bench and got up. "I promised Miss Dobson I'd come and watch the tryouts. I better go talk to her. See you guys later."

She walked away. I leaned over and picked up her lunch bag because I knew Fay wouldn't. In all our years together Missy and I had never seen Fay bring a lunch, but she never asked to share, and she wouldn't scrounge. Plenty of people scrounged, football players especially. But not Fay. Though she would take leftovers rather than let them go to waste.

So I pretended to see if Melissa had left anything in her bag that I'd like, and I said, "This *Brigadoon* thing is really important to her. Dance scholarships and things."

Fay stared stonily at the sandwich in my hand, which I shoved into my coat pocket. When she did speak, it took me by surprise. "She doesn't believe in magic anymore."

"It's not that—" I started, but then I stopped. I just couldn't say anything about lies. *If you play around with little girls who lie, you might become a liar too,* Mrs. Kemble had said to me in fourth grade, her crow voice plenty loud enough for Fay to overhear. *You're a nice girl from a nice home, and your parents have good standards . . .*

That line we'd heard a lot, but it had always been meaningless. My house was too small, and we all hated it, but we couldn't afford to move. And people said it to Melissa, whose parents were divorced.

I handed Melissa's bag to Fay, but she just set it down. Her face was blank, her neck invisible. She looked at me the way she looked back at adults like Mrs. Kemble and Conley the Creep.

I searched for a way to sidestep the subject of lies, to heal the breach, and then I saw it.

"She's making her dream into reality," I said, remembering something Melissa had told me recently. It had sounded like one of those stupid things teachers tell you, like "achieving your goals," but it fit now. "Even when we played those games in the park, you know what her part always was: She had to be the princess, or the shepherd girl, or the witch's kid who saved the prince, or hypnotized a dragon, or saved the world — by dancing."

A brief image lit my mind: Melissa's thin body among the trees, her arms raised and graceful, her long brown hair crowned with a garland of leaves, making her look like something out of Greek mythology and not a real human being. Grown-ups used to stop dead on the paths, watching her.

"Dance is magic for her," I finished. "And all her energy is going into making it *real.*"

"Magic," Fay said in her flattest voice, "already is real. Gandalf said as much in *Lord of the Rings.* But not everyone can see it."

Could I talk about lies without having to say the word?

"But Gandalf isn't real," I said.

"Of course he is. Tolkien believed in Middle Earth," Fay stated. "You can see it in that poem. 'Mythopoeisis.'" She pronounced it carefully, and probably wrong. None of us knew how to say it—the teachers had never heard of the poem. The only poems they seemed to know were ones like "Daffodils."

The bell rang then, startling us both. I was angry with myself for getting sidetracked into arguing whether Middle Earth was real or not when what I wanted was for the three of us to go back to being best friends.

But she stood there stolidly, looking at me with that round, blank face, Melissa's lunch bag sitting forgotten on the bench between us. She said, "Missy doesn't believe me. And you don't either."

So that was that. I walked away, and she didn't call me back.

My next class could have disappeared in a time warp for all I noticed. I sat there staring at my notebook, getting madder by the minute.

I couldn't believe it. Fay wanted me to prove our friendship by believing in lies. No, worse: She was throwing away the friendship for a bunch of lies. Who was that supposed to impress?

In band that afternoon, we sounded terrible.

"Well," Mrs. Lopez said, "since some of you can't seem to find the time to practice at home, we'll use our scheduled hours after school. Report back at three-oh-five."

Everyone else groaned, but as I put my flute away, I was relieved. Now I wouldn't have to see Fay at three. I wouldn't have to do anything about that promise to go to the library.

But after practice, I got a nasty shock.

Mr. Conley was standing there on the steps, as if he hadn't moved since eight A.M. Seeing him, the band members kind of froze up in the doorway, like a clump of zombies.

"Come here." He crooked his finger at me.

The other students swarmed around me like fish in a stream, glad to escape the hook.

"Yes, sir?" My voice quavered. I hated it.

"The United States mail never seems to reach the Reed residence, and they do not possess a telephone. On the chance," he said with heavy sarcasm, "that Mrs. Reed has miraculously recovered from her foot injury, you may deliver this to her while you are consorting with your friend."

And he thrust a sealed envelope into my sweaty hands.

He turned away. I gulped some air in past my pounding heart.

I didn't tell him that I'd never been to Fay's house — didn't even know, except kind of generally, where it was. Nor did I ask why I should do his job for him, especially one (I realized as I looked at the address penciled on the envelope) that would take the rest of the afternoon. You didn't refuse Mr. Conley.

Instead, I went back into the gym and used the public phone to call my mom. "I have to do something for the principal," I said. "I guess I'll be home late."

There was a tiny silence, then of course Mom said, "Well, try to get home before dark."

I thought about everything on the long bus ride across town. If I had any kind of dream, it was to get a long way away from this town and Conley the Creep.

But I had to learn how to deal with the Mr. Conleys of the world.

College was the way, I thought as I leaned my head against the dirty bus window and watched the streets lurch by. I thought about how money was a constant worry in my family; Mom's hours at the flower shop were always getting cut back, and though Dad had recently been promoted to manager at the gas station where he'd always worked, his raise had gone straight into the family fund to take care of Great-Aunt Sarah, who had Alzheimer's.

Reality for my parents was the town where they'd always lived, the jobs they'd always had, the people they'd always known. I wanted more choices, and the ability to make the right ones.

The bus reached the highway outside of town, and I got off. So far I'd managed not to think about what I'd say to Fay if I saw her.

I'd never been asked to Fay's home. Though she, Melissa, and I had been best friends for years, we'd always met at the park, and then at the library. Every year Missy and I invited her to our birthday parties, and Fay always thanked us, but she always had something to do that day. The only two days of the year she was busy.

We hadn't questioned it, it was just the way things were. And considering how much the adults of our town were always complaining about the Reeds — whether Matt, Mark, or Luke, or Charity or Hope or Prudence — it was easier that way than to explain that we were friends with one of the Reeds you didn't hear much about.

Their place was easy to find. One side of the highway was nothing but scrub land, the other a group of rotting buildings, long abandoned. Near a clump of dusty trees squatted a rusting old trailer, with a kind of shed made of battered pieces of sheet metal hammered to the back. Several junker cars rusted around the trash- and weed-choked yard.

I trudged up the rutted dirt road toward the trailer. My heart started hammering when I saw a group of older boys, all tough looking, standing around the engine of an ancient pickup. Nearby, four or five younger kids were playing some kind of game. They were all thick built, like Fay, but some were blonds and some redheads.

They stopped playing when they saw me. "Get lost, buttnugget," a boy yelled at me.

The others laughed; then the big guys looked around.

"Well, hel-lo, baby," one said with a nasty sneer. "Come on over, let's check you out!"

The others greeted this with yells of brainless laughter and disgusting suggestions. Fear choked me; I was ready to drop that envelope and run.

Then a pair of legs appeared from under the car, followed by a muscular torso and a square face and blond hair.

"Shut up," the young man said, and they shut up.

I stared. It was Joseph Reed, the oldest, the only Reed to graduate from high school, though several of them were over eighteen. He was also the only one with a job; he worked, as it happened, for my dad.

He'd never talked to me before, but it was obvious he knew who I was. "Fay's inside, doing homework," he said, pointing a blackened thumb over his shoulder.

I didn't tell him I wasn't there to see Fay. Glad the envelope was in my notebook pressed tight against my chest, I just nodded and went by. The guys were all silent, but I could feel their stares like radiation burns on my back.

Sagging steps led into the open door of the trailer. The first thing that met me was noise from a loud television set. The front door stood wide open, but it did nothing for the thick air inside, which smelled of cigarettes, beer, cooking oil, and hairspray. I stood uncertainly in the doorway, peering into the gloom.

In a corner the TV blared, completely ignored by two huge women, one with bright yellow hair, the other with even brighter red hair. They sat by the kitchen counter, the redhead fixing the blond's hair. Heaped-up ashtrays, dirty dishes, and empty beer cans lay everywhere.

The blond woman raised a beer to her lips, then saw me. Squinting, she said, "You lookin' for someone, sugar?"

"Are you Mrs. Reed?" I asked.

"Depends what you want," she shot back, and both women let loose with loud shrieks of laughter.

"Mr. Conley sent me with this," I said, trying to keep my voice even, as I pulled out the paper. My forehead panged with the beginnings of a headache, and I wondered if Mr. Conley had meant for me to go through this nightmare in order to end a friendship that was already finished.

Mrs. Reed held out her fat hand for the letter. Ripping open the envelope with a long purple nail, she said, "Who are you?"

I didn't want to tell her my name, so I blurted out the next thing that came to me: "I'm in Fay's class."

As soon as it was out I regretted it.

She put her head back, expelling a huge cloud of smoke. "Faith!" she screeched. Then she squinted at the letter and dropped it onto an ashtray on the floor. "Matt again," she said, and laughed.

Then Fay appeared from a back hallway. When she saw me she hunched up, like someone had smacked her.

"I'll be going," I said quickly. "You're busy —"

"Stay awhile." The red-haired woman poked my shoulder, propelling me toward Fay. "Get the kid to talk a little. Ain't natural, sittin' all the time with a book like that."

Fay looked from them to me, then said, "Come on."

The hallway reminded me of an old train: narrow, airless, dark. Trying to find some kind of easy way out, I said, "Are all those your brothers and sisters out there?"

I didn't even know how many of them there were. Too late I realized the question might seem an insult.

"Some. Rest are cousins," she said, still in that flat voice. "That's my Aunt Leah out front."

"Does everybody have Bible names?" I thought that, at least, would be safe to ask, as she pushed aside a hanging beach towel in a doorway.

Inside was a tiny room with four futons on the floor. Most of the room was an even worse mess than the living room, except for one corner. There three plastic boxes stuffed with neatly folded clothes stood next to a tidily made-up futon. On the top of the crates sat an old, cracked radio, propping up a row of library books.

Fay's radio, I realized. Her bed, her clothes. Her books.

She turned around and faced me, her arms crossed. "Grandma named us," she said, still flat as cement. "Ma not being married, Gran paid for the hospital, so long's she could name us. Had us all baptized, too. Anything else you want to know?"

Her anger made mine come rushing back. If her magic was so real, then why was she living in this disgusting dump? The tiniest spell could at least empty an ashtray. "Is that the radio where you listened to Middle Earth?" I asked, pointing.

Fay's cheeks showed dull red, but just as her mouth opened, a set of clicking claws ticked right up behind me, and I got thumped in the back by a stout dog with a shaggy tan coat.

He slobbered onto my hand, which I snatched away and wiped on my coat. I asked, "Is this the one that talks?"

The dog bounded past me to Fay, jumping up with his paws on her chest.

She grabbed his paws and held him, though the dog must have weighed at least as much as she did. Looking him right in the muzzle, she said: "C'mon, Aslan, tell her hello."

I felt like someone had doused me with ice water.

He dropped down, panting, his tongue lolling out, and thumped his tail. She glanced up at me once, then bent close to him. "Please. Say something."

She's crazy, I thought, backing up a step. She's a crazy girl living with a lot of horrible crazy people, and I never knew it.

A sudden gulping sob stopped me in my retreat. Fay buried her face in the dog's dirty ruff. "Talk," she cried into his fur. "Talk. Please, Aslan. Please." And she cried, not noisily like a baby, but the terrible soundless crying of a person who has lost everything, her whole body shaking.

I stood there, my anger gone. Now what do I do?

I looked at Fay, who crouched on her futon, still holding the dog. He sat patiently under her tight grip, his tail stirring as he looked up at me.

This is Fay's reality, I thought. No wonder she believes in magic. A great wave of pity swept through me, piling up behind my teeth and tongue, but I didn't say anything, because I knew, as surely as I knew she had never come to our birthday parties, had never asked to share our lunches, that Fay would hate pity.

I dropped onto my knees at the other end of the futon and held out a hand to the dog. Maybe I couldn't say anything, but could I, like, show her how sorry I was?

Her head was still buried in the dog's fur. I looked past her, wondering what I could do or say. My eyes lit on that radio, and I remembered all those Middle Earth reports. How much Missy and I had loved those stories. Heck, how believable they had been — true to the characters, as if J.R.R. Tolkien himself had made them up.

This *isn't* her reality, I thought. She's made a reality all for herself, filled with magical happenings and interesting people and faraway places. And in its own way, it's just as real as Missy's dream to dance with the New York Ballet.

My pity was gone. In its place were admiration and envy. The radio, the dog, even the trailer — I remembered once in fifth grade, she told us that her house could fly. Trailers moved, and with a little imagination, maybe it could fly. She'd taken bits of her horrible life and made it fun.

"It doesn't matter," I said. "I believe you, Fay. I believe you."

She lifted her head, just a bit. Her red eyes were more suspicious than anything else.

I threw my arms wide. "You're right," I said. "I've been thinking, and you're totally, absolutely *right,* that magic *can* be found if a person looks hard enough. I'm sorry I was blind."

She gave a long sniff and sat up, knuckling her eyes. "Wh-what made you ch-ange your mind?" Her breathing was still ragged.

"There is magic here," I said. "I can feel it."

She gave another sob, but it was the relief kind, the storm-is-over kind. The dog thrust his muzzle under my hand, then sniffed at my coat pocket, where the ham sandwich had sat all afternoon, forgotten.

I patted the dog's head absently, smiling at Fay. At last, she smiled back.

"Food!" the dog barked, looking from one of us to the other. "More food! Food!"

About the Authors

DAN BENNETT writes features and medical stories for a daily newspaper in Fort Smith, Arkansas. His first published story, "Maggie," appeared in the final issue of *The Twilight Zone Magazine*. He shares a palatial one-bedroom apartment with a computer and a dangerous black cat.

BRUCE COVILLE is the popular author of many books, including *Jeremy Thatcher, Dragon Hatcher* and *Jennifer Murdley's Toad,* and the bestselling *My Teacher Is an Alien*. He edited *The Unicorn Treasury* and *Herds of Thunder, Manes of Gold*. "Fantasy at its best" is how *Publisher's Weekly* describes his work. He was an elementary schoolteacher for many years before becoming a full-time writer and has also worked as a grave digger, a toy maker, an air freight agent, and a movie actor. He lives with his wife and two of their three children in Syracuse, New York, where he was born.

CHARLES DE LINT is the author of *The Dreaming Place, Spiritwalk,* and *The Little Country* — for which he was nominated for the World Fantasy Award — as well as a dozen other novels. He writes high fantasy, urban fantasy, horror, and young-adult fiction. He and his wife, MaryAnn Harris, make their home in Ottawa, Canada, where both can be found at local sessions playing Celtic music.

DEBRA DOYLE AND JAMES D. MACDONALD, an Ivy League Ph.D. and an ex-naval officer respectively, have been married since 1978 and writing together since 1986. Since then they have published numerous books, including a series of middle grade fantasy novels known collectively as *Circle of Magic,* and the first two volumes of a science fiction series called Mageworlds: *The Price of the Stars* and *Starpilot's Grave.* They live in Colebrook, New Hampshire, with their four children, two cats, and a passel of computers.

TAPPAN KING is the author of a number of short stories and several novels, including the young adult fantasy novel *Down Town,* coauthored with Viido Polikarpus, and the forthcoming science fiction novel *Escape Velocity.* He has been an editor for Bantam Books and *The Twilight Zone Magazine,* as well as a consultant to the publishing and computer industries. He and his wife, editor Beth Meacham, live in Tucson, Arizona.

BETTY LEVIN is the author of a great many children's books and novels, including *The Sword of Culann, Landfall, A Beast on the Brink, The Keeping-Room,* and most recently, *Mercy's Mill.* In addition to writing and teaching she runs a sheep farm in Lincoln, Massachusetts.

JOY OESTREICHER has been a secretary, tariff clerk, administrator, research assistant, dress designer, tailor, shipping clerk, photographer's aide, astrologer, tax preparation assistant, model, and Girl Scout leader. She edits and publishes the small poetry magazine *Xenophilia,* and the speculative-fiction anthology *Air Fish.* Her 2.5 children are now outnumbered by cats.

WILL SHETTERLY has written six fantasy novels, including *Elsewhere* and *Nevernever,* as well as the forthcoming *Dogland.* With his wife, the novelist Emma Bull, he has edited a series of short-story anthologies set in the magical world of Liavek. He is also the publisher of Steeldragon Press, which issues limited-edition books and comic books, as well as recordings of the rock band Cats Laughing. He and his wife live in Minneapolis.

ALAN P. SMALE is an astrophysicist and works in the Laboratory for High Energy Astrophysics at the Goddard Space Flight Center. He lives in Bowie, Maryland, with his wife, Karen. Though he has published a large number of scientific papers, this is his first published short story.

SHERWOOD SMITH began making books when she was only five years old, taping paper towels together and illustrating the stories with crayons. Since then she has gone on to write and publish several popular books, including *Wren to the Rescue, Wren's Quest,* and the forthcoming *Wren's War,* as well as the science fiction novel *The Phoenix in Flight,* coauthored with Dave Trowbridge.

VIVIAN VANDE VELDE is the author of five fantasy novels, including *Dragon's Bait* and *User Unfriendly,* both published by Jane Yolen Books. Her short stories have appeared in numerous magazines, including *Cricket, Aboriginal Science Fiction,* and *Isaac Asimov's Science Fiction Magazine.* She lives in Rochester, New York, with her husband, Jim, and their daughter.

PATRICIA C. WREDE is the author of nearly a dozen fantasy novels, including the four novels of the Enchanted Forest Chronicles: *Dealing with Dragons, Searching for Dragons, Calling on Dragons,* and *Talking to Dragons.* She lives in Edina, a suburb of Minneapolis.

JANE YOLEN is the author of some one hundred and fifty books for adults and children, including *Wizard's Hall, Tam Lin,* and *The Devil's Arithmetic.* Her most recent adult fantasy, *Briar Rose,* was nominated for the Nebula Award — her third consecutive novel to be given that honor. Among her many awards are the Regina Medal, the World Fantasy Award, the Kerlan Award, and, for her book *Owl Moon,* the Caldecott Medal in 1988. She lives with her husband, David Stemple, in Hatfield, Massachusetts.